W9-AVO-203

LEAVING EPITAPH

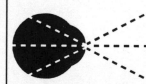

This Large Print Book carries the
Seal of Approval of N.A.V.H.

THE SONS OF DANIEL SHAYE

LEAVING EPITAPH

ROBERT J. RANDISI

THORNDIKE PRESS

A part of Gale, Cengage Learning

GALE
CENGAGE Learning·

Farmington Hills, Mich • San Francisco • New York • Waterville, Maine
Meriden, Conn • Mason, Ohio • Chicago

GALE
CENGAGE Learning®

LIBRARY OF CONGRESS CATALOGING-IN-PUBLICATION DATA

Randisi, Robert J.
    Leaving Epitaph : the sons of Daniel Shaye / by Robert J. Randisi. — Large
Print edition.
        pages cm. — (Thorndike Press Large Print Western)
    ISBN 978-1-4104-6695-2 (hardcover) — ISBN 1-4104-6695-7 (hardcover)
    1. Texas—Fiction. 2. Large type books. I. Title.
PS3568.A53L43 2014
813'.54—dc23   2013047043

Published in 2014 by arrangement with Harper, an imprint of
HarperCollins Publishers

Printed in the United States of America
1 2 3 4 5 6 7 18 17 16 15 14

To the sons of Bob Randisi

1

He never expected that a handful of dirt striking the top of a coffin would make such a loud sound.

Daniel Shaye stepped back from his wife's open grave to allow his three sons to approach. One at a time they opened their hands and let the dirt fall. Each time it sounded loud as a drum to Shaye.

The three boys stepped back and stood abreast of their father, and the four of them folded their hands in front of them. As the townspeople filed by them, offering their condolences, the four men stood like stone. No one in the town had done a thing while Ethan Langer and his gang had ridden Mary Shaye down in the street while making their escape after robbing the bank. Neither her husband nor any of her sons would ever forgive them for that.

The last to approach them was the reverend.

"You can't hold these good people responsible for what happened, Daniel," Reverend Henry Mitchell said.

"Why not, Reverend?" Shaye asked.

"It was not their job to try and stop those bank robbers."

"Job?" Shaye asked. "Who's talking about a job, Reverend? They had a moral obligation to try to help my wife. Any sort of action might have caused that gang to stop, or swerve, or change direction. Mary was just crossing the street, carrying a bolt of fabric in her arms, and those animals trampled her into the dirt. That was no way for a woman to die — no way for my wife to die. It was senseless."

"Still —"

"Save your breath, Reverend." Thomas Shaye, at twenty-five, was the oldest of the three sons. Physically, however, he resembled his mother, favoring her slighter frame over his father's powerful one. "Ain't none of us listenin'."

"We wouldn't be listenin' if God Hisself was talkin'," said James, nineteen.

"That's blasphemy, boy," the reverend said sternly, but he took a step back when twenty-three-year-old Matthew, the largest of the boys, spoke.

"It was blasphemy what happened to our

8

maw, Reverend!" he snapped. "If there even was a God, why would He let that happen?"

Henry Mitchell had been the reverend in Epitaph, Texas, for thirteen years. He'd known Daniel Shaye and his family since they moved to town twelve years ago. He not only considered himself the keeper of their souls, but he thought of Daniel Shaye as a good friend.

He recovered his composure and said to Daniel, "You should tell your boys not to blaspheme the Lord, Dan —"

"My wife is dead, Henry," Dan Shaye said, cutting him off. "You think I care what you or the Lord thinks?"

"You're all grieving," Mitchell said. "I know you don't mean what you're saying —"

"Reverend," Daniel Shaye said, "when have you ever known me not to mean what I say? And I raised my boys the same way. We speak our minds, and right now we don't have God in our minds, or in our hearts."

"What then? Vengeance?" Mitchell asked.

"You bet," Shaye said.

"As sheriff of Epitaph it's your job to capture those men, and bring the money they stole back to town, Daniel," Mitchell said. "Vengeance should have nothing to do with that."

"It's my job to catch 'em, Reverend," Shaye said, "but it's gonna be my pleasure to kill 'em."

With that he turned and walked away from his wife's grave. They had chosen to bury her out in a field behind their house, and not on Boot Hill with all the others. He had not wanted his loving wife to be buried with any of those miscreants on the hill.

Thomas, Matthew, and James Shaye all gave the reverend one last, hard look and then turned and followed their father back to the house.

The boys found their father standing in front of the cold fireplace, staring, arms folded. They exchanged anxious looks, but none of them said a word for several moments. When their father failed to acknowledge them, Thomas finally took it upon himself to break the silence.

"Pa?"

Shaye didn't answer.

"Pa?" Thomas said again.

"Boys," Shaye said, without turning.

"What are we gonna do, Pa?" Thomas asked.

Daniel Shaye moved one hand, passed it across his face, then refolded his arms again.

"I'm going after the gang," he finally said.

"Alone?" Thomas asked.

"With a posse."

"It's been three days, Pa," Matthew said.

"That's okay, Matthew," Shaye said. "I'll find them."

"Can we come, Pa?" James asked.

Now Shaye turned to face his sons. "No."

"But Pa —" Thomas said.

"No," Shaye said again, sternly. "Your mother would never forgive me if anything happened to you boys."

"Ma's dead, Pa," Thomas said. "We've got to do somethin'."

"I know that, Thomas," Shaye said. "The answer is still no."

"Pa —" James started.

"The discussion is over."

He turned and faced the fireplace again. The boys looked at each other and remained silent, but they knew the discussion was not over.

2

The day after his wife was buried, Sheriff Daniel Shaye stood across the desk from Mayor Charles Garnett.

"The town wants to know when you're going after the gang, Dan," Garnett said.

"Worried about their money, are they?"

"Yes, they're very worried about their money," the mayor said. "Most of the town had their money in the bank, Dan. Jesus, this is 1889, for Chrissake. There's not supposed to be bank robbers anymore."

Shaye stared at the florid-faced mayor, a big man in his fifties whose face always shone red when he was distressed.

"If the town's so concerned, Mayor, then how come no one will volunteer for a posse?"

Mayor Garnett sat back in his chair. "You want the honest truth, Dan?"

"Honesty would be a nice change, coming from a politician, Charlie," Shaye said.

"I don't think I deserved that."

Shaye did not reply.

"They're afraid of you, Dan."

"What?"

"It's been four days since Mary's . . . since Mary died, only one since she was buried," Garnett explained. "The whole town turned out for her funeral, and all they felt from you was hate."

"Where was the whole town when the Langer gang rode Mary down, Charlie?"

"I've talked with the reverend, Dan," Garnett said. "You can't blame the whole town for that. That was the Langer gang. Blame them. Hate them. Go after them."

"I am going after them, Charlie," Shaye said, "with or without a posse."

"What about your deputies?"

"They quit."

"Did they say why?"

"They didn't say a word," Shaye answered. "I found their badges on my desk this morning."

"They're afraid of you too, Dan."

"What about you, Mayor?" Shaye asked. "Are you also afraid of me?"

Garnett hesitated, then said, "A little. I've never seen you like this, Dan. I've never seen a man so filled with . . . rage. You . . . you . . . vibrate with it. Containing it seems

13

to take all your strength. I don't think anyone wants to be around when it comes out."

"The only ones who have to fear that is the Langer gang."

"It's been four days," Garnett said. "They're getting farther and farther away with our money."

"Is that all you're worried about, Mayor?" Shaye asked. "All you're concerned with? The money?"

"Of course not, Dan," Garnett said. "We want them brought to justice for what they did to Mary, but be realistic. You can't bring Mary back, but you can bring them — and the money — back."

For a moment Mayor Garnett thought he'd gone too far. That barely contained rage he'd seen before flared in Dan Shaye's eyes and then subsided.

"Dan," Charlie Garnett said, "we're friends. We've been friends for twelve years, since you and Mary brought the boys here and you took the job as sheriff. I think I should be able to speak freely here."

Shaye hesitated, then said, "Go ahead."

"I think," Garnett said, very carefully, "what you're feeling is not so much anger as guilt."

"Over what?"

"You weren't there when Mary . . . when the gang hit the bank. You didn't get there in time to stop them, or to save her."

"I was at the other end of town, Mayor," Shaye said, "doing my job."

"I know that, Dan," Garnett said, "and so do you. There was nothing you could have done."

"Oh, but there was," Shaye said. "If I'd been there I could have stopped them."

"All eight of them?"

"I would have stopped them," Shaye said again. "I would have kept Mary alive."

"Dan —"

"Charlie," Shaye said, cutting the man off, "I'm going after that gang even if I have to go alone. I'm going to kill them, one by one —"

"Dan," Garnett said, "that's not your job —"

"— and if they still have the money, I'll bring it back here," Shaye went on, not giving the mayor a chance to finish. "But understand this: My first duty is to my dead wife, and to my sons, to avenge their mother's death. My duty is not to a town that stood by and watched her die, or who will stand by now and not volunteer to lift a finger to help hunt them down."

"They're storekeepers, Dan," Garnett

15

said, "not manhunters."

"No," Shaye said, "that's me. I'm the manhunter, and that's what I'm going to do. Hunt them down."

"Alone."

"Yes, if I have to," Shaye said. "What I need to know is, do you want this badge back?"

"If I take that badge, then you'll have no authority to hunt them," Garnett said. "You'll be no better than a bounty hunter."

"That's right."

"I won't do that to you, Dan," Garnett said. "I told you, we're friends. You keep the badge, and you find somebody to pin those deputies' badges on. The town will be with you in spirit and goodwill —"

"This town can take its spirit and goodwill and stick it up its collective ass, Charlie," Shaye said. "And that includes you."

Charlie Garnett spread his beefy hands and said, "If I could even still sit a horse, I'd be right with you, Dan —"

"Save it, Charlie," Shaye said. "You're all alike, all of you storekeepers and politicians." He turned, stalked over to the door, opened it, then stood there with his hand on the knob. "I'll be leaving in the morning. I'll outfit myself from the general store. I assume the town will foot the bill?"

16

"Of course. It's the least we can do."

"It's the very least you will do, Charlie."

"Dan —"

Shaye stopped with one foot out the door. "What?"

"What are you going to do for deputies?"

"I don't know, Charlie," Shaye said, "but with or without deputies or a posse, I'm leaving in the morning."

As Sheriff Daniel Shaye walked out the door, slamming it behind him, Mayor Charles Garnett thought that, one way or another, he would never see Shaye again.

3

On the street in front of City Hall, Dan Shaye stopped and stood on the boardwalk. People walked past him and lowered their eyes, not wanting to meet his. He had thought for years that they were his friends, his wife's friends, but the events of the past few days had proven him wrong. They were not his friends. He was the sheriff, and they were the town, and there would always be a barrier between them.

He stepped into the street and crossed over, headed for his office. He knew his days as sheriff of Epitaph were numbered. He needed the badge only to give him some semblance of authority while he hunted the gang, even though he was sure to end up out of his jurisdiction. After that, from wherever he ended up, he'd send it back to them.

He'd spent the better part of the day trying to replace his deputies or round up a posse, and had failed at both. Now there was only one course of action left to him.

When he reached his office, he opened the door and stepped inside. He found three men waiting for him, and they were all wearing deputy's badges.

"Hello, boys," he said to his three sons.

Earlier in the day the three boys had talked while at the house, which was situated at the south end of town. They had spent the past twelve years there, but now it felt oddly empty.

"What are we gonna do, Thomas?" James asked his older brother. "We can't just let Pa go after those men without us."

"He ain't gonna get a posse up," Matthew said. "And his deputies have already quit."

Matthew had gone to town earlier in the day to get some idea of what was happening, and had returned with this news.

"There's only one thing we can do, boys," Thomas said. "We got to be Pa's deputies."

"He used to call us that, when I was little," James said. "His little deputies, remember?"

"I remember," Matthew said. "Ma used to tell him not to even think about it."

"Well," Thomas said, "he's gonna have to think about it now, 'cause we're all he's got. And we got a right to avenge Ma's death, just as much as he has."

"Even me?" James asked hopefully.

"Even you, James," Thomas said. "You're a man growed, just like we are."

"So what do we do, Thomas?" Matthew asked.

"We go to town," Thomas said, "and we don't give Pa a choice."

"We stand up to him?" Matthew asked.

"That's what we do."

"We ain't never done that before," James said.

"Well, we're gonna have to do it now," Thomas said. "We got to be together on this. Matthew?"

The middle brother took a moment to think, then nodded and said, "Yes."

"James?"

"Oh, yes," the younger brother said without hesitation.

"Then let's go to town, boys."

The three boys had just pinned on the badges they'd found on top of and inside the desk when their father walked into the office.

"What have we here?" he asked.

"Deputies, Pa," Thomas said.

"Three of us," Matthew said.

"We heard what was happening in town," James said. "You need us, Pa."

20

"And we deserve to go along," Thomas said. "She was our mother. We got a right to avenge her death."

Dan Shaye studied his three sons. They all stood as tall as he, Matthew even taller and bigger. They all wore guns. He knew that Thomas could shoot. He knew that Matthew's size and strength made him deadly in a fight. James was nineteen, though. He could not shoot like his older brother, nor could he fight like Matthew. But he had the same rights as the other two boys.

"Pa?" Thomas said.

"My three deputies," Shaye said. "Your mother would kill me for pinning those badges on you."

"You didn't pin 'em on us," Thomas pointed out.

"We pinned 'em on ourselves," James added.

"Yeah," Dan Shaye said, "yeah, you did."

In truth, Shaye had already decided that his only course of action was to take his sons along, after first deputizing them. They had never gone against another man in a fight, never killed another man, but he had no choice. If he was going to catch up to the Langer gang and make them pay for what they had done to Mary Shaye, he couldn't go alone.

21

"You boys have to do what I say, when I say."

"We will, Pa," Thomas said.

"Every step of the way," Shaye added, "no questions asked."

"We will," Matthew said.

"James?"

"Yeah, Pa?"

"You'll have to do the cooking."

James smiled and said, "Right, Pa."

Shaye stepped forward and spread his arms wide. The three boys stepped forward and all four embraced briefly, but powerfully.

"Let's go and get outfitted, then," Shaye said. "Like somebody just told me, it's the least this town can do."

4

The Shaye men spent the rest of the day outfitting themselves with clothing, weapons, food, and horses. In every store they entered they received nothing but co-operation, but no one dared look any of them in the eye.

The clothing they bought had to be good for warm or cold weather, whichever way the trail took them. The food had to be carried between them, because Shaye didn't want any pack animals slowing them down. Jerky, bacon, and beans would make up their diet for as long as the hunt took.

Shaye allowed the boys to go and buy the clothing and food without him, but he accompanied them to buy weapons and horses. Thomas carried a new Peacemaker and was able to shoot very well with it. Matthew had an old Navy Colt, and James did not have a gun of his own. Shaye obtained for Matthew and James guns identical to their older brother's, and they all got the newest model Winchester. All four of them got a new horse for the hunt, picked more for stamina than speed. None of the boys complained about leaving their own horses behind.

"The hunt" was what they were calling it. They did not pretend that it was anything but, because when you hunted, it was understood that you intended to kill your prey.

"I want the three of you to understand something," Shaye said to his sons later that night, when they were in the Red Garter Saloon. Their presence had killed business for the night, since no one wanted to be in the same room with them — not after the funeral and the sheriff's unsuccessful attempt to gather a posse. The only other people in the place were the bartender and two saloon girls.

"What's that, Pa?" Matthew asked.

"We're not going after these men to bring them back," Shaye said. "We're going after them to kill them."

"Won't that get you in trouble?" James asked. "I mean, you bein' the law an' all?"

"It could get us all in trouble," Shaye admitted. "We're all representing the law, but more than that, we're representing the

24

husband and sons of Mary Shaye. In my book, that's even more important."

"To us too, Pa," Thomas assured him.

"You haven't killed anyone, you haven't even ever shot at anyone," Shaye said. "That's all going to change."

"We know that, Pa," Matthew said.

"Are you ready for it?"

"Sure we are," James said enthusiastically.

"I don't think you are," Shaye said, filling four shot glasses with rye from a bottle he was holding, "but by the time we catch up to them, you will be, because you're all going to get your education on the trail."

He picked up his glass and his sons emulated him.

"Here's to the memory of Mary Shaye," the father said, and the sons lifted their glasses and joined him in downing his toast.

"Now you boys better get off to bed," Shaye said. "No more drinking tonight. You've got to be sharp in the morning."

"What about you, Pa?" Thomas asked.

"I'll be along," Shaye said. "Go on, do as I say."

Thomas stood and his brother followed his lead. As they went out the door, Shaye poured himself another glass of rye.

Later Dan Shaye stood in the moonlight at his wife's grave, still holding the bottle.

"I have to take them with me, Mary," he said to his dead wife, "if only because I don't know if I'll be coming back. I sure have a better chance of coming back with them than without them, though, don't I?"

He took a drink from the bottle and then tossed it away, still half full. He wasn't foolish enough to get drunk the night before the hunt started.

"I'd swear to God that I'll try my best to keep them safe, but I'm kind of mad at God right now, so I'll just give you my promise. I'll keep them safe, and I'll kill the murdering bastards who took you from us."

With the promise offered and — he hoped — accepted, he turned and walked to the house where he and his sons would spend the night for perhaps the last time.

The next morning the four Shaye men split the supplies evenly among them and mounted their horses in front of the livery stable.

"Where we headed, Pa?" James asked.

"North," Shaye said. "They headed north."

"Why not south, to Mexico?" Matthew asked.

"Because Ethan Langer doesn't run and hide after he hits a bank," Shaye said. "He

26

joins up with his brother Aaron, after he and his men also hit a bank."

"You mean they hit banks in different towns at the same time?" Thomas asked.

"Roughly the same time," Shaye said. "I got a telegram yesterday from the sheriff up in Prairie Bend, South Dakota, that the Langer gang hit their bank yesterday. It's a competition between them, I think, to see who gets more money."

"Is that sheriff tracking them?" James asked.

"Won't go out of his jurisdiction."

"So where will they go?" Matthew asked.

"Aaron and his part of the gang will go south, while Ethan and his part will go north. They'll probably meet up somewhere in Kansas."

"So we're goin' to Kansas?" James asked.

"We're going north," Shaye said. "Wherever they end up, that's where we'll end up."

5

Ethan Langer poured himself a cup of coffee and replaced the pot without offering any of his men some. Terry Petry picked up the pot and filled his own cup. The other men were too busy eating to notice or care what was going on with the coffee.

"Whataya think, Ethan?" Petry asked. "We do better than Aaron and the boys?"

"We won't know till we meet up," Langer said.

"Yeah, I know, but whataya guess?"

"I don't guess, Terry," Langer said. "I never guess. I pick my banks because it's where I know we'll do the best. Aaron picks his the same way. We'll see who got the most when we meet up, like always."

"Okay, sure," Petry said, "sure, Ethan."

Langer drank his coffee and avoided looking into the fire. He'd had one plate of bacon and beans and that had been enough. Despite what he told Petry, he was wondering how his brother Aaron had done in South Dakota. He hated going north himself, because he hated the cold. That's why most of the jobs he'd pulled over the past year had been in Texas, New Mexico, and Arizona.

"Too bad about the woman," Petry said.

"Huh?"

"That woman that we rode down," the other man said. "Too bad she was in the street."

"Stupid bitch got what she deserved," Langer said.

"Wonder who she was?"

"Who cares?" Langer demanded. "Look, Petry, go and sit at the other fire, okay? Yer startin' to piss me off."

There were two campfires for the eight men, and they were sitting four and four, but now Langer took out his gun and waved it around.

"All of ya, go sit by the other fire, damn it! Now!"

Petry and the other men moved quickly, so that there were now seven men seated around the other fire. Ethan Langer was known to have a short fuse. A big man, he dealt out punishment with his fists or his gun, and none of the men wanted to risk either.

Langer holstered his gun and poured himself more coffee. What did he care what happened to some stupid woman who was standing in the street? Goddamn dumb bitch was too slow-witted to move, she deserved to get ridden down. His horse had been the first to strike her, and the shocked look on her face was still vivid in his mind. So vivid that he had been seeing it in his sleep every night since then.

Goddamn bitch, she'd haunted him all the way here to the Oklahoma Territory. How much longer did she intend to haunt him?

6

When Dan Shaye and his sons rode into Vernon, Texas, a week after leaving Epitaph they were all bearded except for James, whose cheeks had only been able to sprout some fuzz during that time.

The young men had learned a lot from their father during that week: much about tracking, like reading sign. They now knew that when you were tracking someone, the evidence of their passing was not just on the ground, but in broken branches, as well, or places where branches and brush had been gathered for a fire. They had also learned about the proper care of a horse while on the trail — how important it was to walk a horse at times, resting it but not necessarily stopping your progress — and of making and breaking camp. James had been taught to cook by his mother, but on this trip he'd learned a thing or two about trail coffee from his father.

31

They'd learned about shooting too. Every day after they ate, Dan Shaye had schooled his boys on the proper use of a handgun and a rifle. Thomas, though a fair hand with a pistol, had never drawn or fired the weapon at another man. Shaye taught them where to shoot a man to be sure to bring him down, and what to do when facing a man who was better than they were with a gun. He explained that it was not the fastest man with a gun who survived, but the most accurate.

After one particular lesson, James had said, "But, Pa, that wouldn't be fair."

"You want to be fair, boy?" Shaye had asked him. "Or alive?"

The answer was easy for all three boys.

Along the trail the three young men had time alone with their own thoughts, both on horseback and at night, when they were camped. Shaye made them all stand watch, made sure they all knew not to stare into the fire and destroy their night vision, but there was plenty of time for introspection.

Thomas was normally a quiet person, so introspection was nothing new to him. Growing up, he often went off alone to shoot targets and think. He wanted very much to be like his father, even though his physical resemblance was to his mother. At six feet tall, he was a slender 170, and he had a good eye and fast hands. He'd asked his father on more than one occasion to make him a deputy, but his mother had always stepped in and vetoed the idea.

"I worry day and night about your father," she'd say, "I'm not going to do the same with you or any of my boys."

Those first seven nights on the trail, Thomas thought about those words, and now it wasn't any of them who was dead, but her. He felt guilty that it had taken the death of his mother to get him the job he wanted — deputy to his father, whom he considered not only a great lawman, but a great man as well.

The middle brother, Matthew, was not much for thinking. At six-five, he was three inches taller than his father, but he resembled him more than either of the other two boys. He had his father's breadth of chest and shoulders, and was narrow in the waist, the way Dan Shaye had been before he moved into his forties. Now forty-eight, Shaye had thickened somewhat, but still had his power, though less than his middle son's, and for that he was proud rather than envious.

While on the trail, Matthew had done some thinking, and had posed many questions to himself. He would follow his father to hell and back, but he wondered what was going to happen when it was all over.

He had no doubt that he and his brothers would follow their father and be successful in killing the men who had taken their mother from them. But what then?

Would his father go back to being sheriff of Epitaph?

Would he and his brothers stay on as deputies?

Would they live in the same house?

He knew there was danger in what they were doing, but he had so much confidence in his father that he felt no fear.

In his father's eyes, this was not a good thing.

James loved his father, but he idolized his oldest brother, the way many younger brothers did. Like his older brother, he resembled his mother more than his father, and so when the four men were together, Shaye and Matthew looked like big hulking brutes, while Thomas and James were slender and graceful. James was impressed with the way Thomas handled a gun, and hoped that someday he'd be able to do the same. During the target shooting they'd done while on the trail, he had begun to display certain natural abilities with a handgun, but he still had a long way to go to match Thomas — and they both had far to go to be ready to face another man with a gun.

James missed his mother terribly, but felt that he was on a great adventure with his father and brothers, and he hoped that the adventure would not only continue, but escalate.

Like his brother Matthew, James felt no fear.

Thomas, on the other hand, was worried about his father and his two brothers, was afraid that something might happen to them. But he worried little about himself. For someone who had never faced another man with a gun, he was inordinately confident.

For his part, Dan Shaye worried about all his sons. Thomas was too confident, Matthew too brave, and James too headstrong and adventurous. He knew that all of these qualities would have to be tempered with his own experience — and yet could he keep a tight rein on his boys *and* his own rage?

By the time they rode into Vernon, Texas,

all of the Shaye men had had their share of deep thoughts. Also, though they hadn't met the Langer gang, they came upon their trail in two other towns, which told them they were on the right track.

"How long we stayin', Pa?" James asked.

"How long do you want to stay, James?"

"Well," the younger Shaye said, rubbing his face, "long enough for a shave, maybe. I'm startin' to itch."

Matthew, who had the heaviest beard of the four, reached out and touched James's face.

"You got nothin' but peach fuzz there, little brother," he said, laughing. "Why don't you wait until you got a man's full growth of beard before you complain?"

James brushed Matthew's tree trunk arm away from him, while Thomas had a good laugh.

"I have to talk to the local law," Shaye said, "and it's a few hours from dark. We'll stay the night, and you boys can all get a shave and a bath."

"A bath!" Matthew said, appalled. "Why would we want to take a bath, Pa?"

"Because, Matthew," James said, "some of us smell like a goat."

Matthew squinted his eyes at his younger brother and said, "You wouldn't be talkin' about me, would you, little brother?"

"You all smell like goats," Shaye said, "and so do I. Take your horses to the livery, be sure they're fed and bedded down, and then get us two rooms at the hotel. Thomas, you'll be in a room with me."

"Yes, Pa."

"And you're in charge of these two," Shaye went on. "After you get the rooms, see that they're bathed, shaved, and that they keep out of trouble."

"Yes, Pa. . . . Pa?"

"What?"

"Do you know the local lawman here?"

"Yes," Shay said. "He's an old friend of mine, name of Sam Torrence."

"I heard you mention him. Weren't you deputies together?"

"Years ago, boy," Shaye said, "a lot of years ago."

"Want us to take your horse, Pa?" James asked.

"I'll take care of my animal," Shaye said, "you boys take care of your own."

"Yes, sir."

"I'll meet you back at the hotel in two hours."

"Two hours?" Matthew complained. "That's barely time to see to our horses and have a bath and a shave."

"And no time to get into trouble," Shaye said. "That's about what I had in mind, boy."

7

When Dan Shaye entered the sheriff's office, the man behind the desk looked up from the wanted posters he was studying, frowned just for a moment, then smiled and stood up.

"Dan Shaye!" Sam Torrence said, extending his hand. "What the hell are you doing in Vernon? I didn't think you ever left South Texas anymore."

"Hello, Sam," Shaye said. He approached the desk and shook hands with the tall, slender man whose hair had gone completely gray since the last time Shaye had seen him.

"It's good to see you, Dan," Torrence said. "What brings you my way?"

"The Langer gang."

"I heard they hit a bank down south," Torrence said. "That was you?"

Shaye nodded, then said, "They killed my wife during their escape."

"Ah, Jesus . . ." Torrence's face went pale. "Mary . . ."

"Rode her down in the street, Sam."

"Christ," Torrence said. "Sit down, Dan. I was gonna offer you some coffee but this is better."

He brought a bottle of whiskey out of his desk drawer, then fetched two coffee cups from the potbellied stove in the corner. He poured a shot into each and handed one to Shaye.

"Here's to Mary," he said.

"To Mary."

They both drank, and when Torrence reached across the desk to pour again, Shaye placed his cup on the desk, upside down.

"One's enough for me."

"Not for me," Torrence said. He poured another shot and downed it. "You on their trail?"

Shaye nodded.

"With a posse."

"My boys."

"Your . . ."

"Sons," Shaye said. "Three of 'em."

"That's right," Torrence said, snapping his fingers, "I knew you and Mary had three sons. How old are they?"

"Twenty-five, twenty-three, and nineteen.

I deputized them."

"Are they experienced?"

"No," Shaye said, "but I had no choice. No one else volunteered, my deputies quit. Besides, they deserve to come. Langer and his boys killed their ma."

"We're talkin' about Ethan Langer, right?"

"Yeah," Shaye said. "Aaron hit a bank in South Dakota about the same time."

"So you're trackin' them north . . . through here?"

"You tell me, Sam."

Torrence sat back in his chair, which creaked. "They ain't been through here, Dan," he said, shaking his head. "I'd know if they had."

Shaye stood up. "We'll be here overnight, Sam, and then we'll be moving out. If you have anything you want to tell me, you'll be able to find me."

"Dan," Torrence said, "I'm tellin' you —"

"It's good to see you, Sam."

Shaye turned and walked out of the office. He knew that Torrence's eyes were on his back. He stopped just outside the door, in case the other lawman came after him right away.

The last time Shaye saw Torrence had been years ago, before he moved on to wear the sheriff's badge in Epitaph. They had both been in Wichita, and Shaye had caught Torrence with his hand out. All these years later there was no reason to think the man had changed. A lawman with his hand out could live very well, and Shaye had the feeling Torrence was doing all right for himself in Vernon. However, if he had taken a dime from Ethan Langer and was covering up for him, he would regret it.

8

In a nearby bathhouse, Thomas Shaye was drying off, while both Matthew and James were still languishing in tubs of what was now tepid water.

"Hey, this ain't half bad," Matthew said.

"I can see why," Thomas said. "You've got enough mud and dirt floating in that water to satisfy any pig."

"You sayin' I'm a pig, Thomas?" Matthew asked.

Their mother had given them names from the Bible, and had never shortened them. They were forever Thomas, Matthew, and James, never Tommy, Matt, or Jimmy.

"Would I call you that, Matthew?" Thomas asked. "I'm just commentin' on your dirty water."

Matthew looked down at his bathwater and made a face. "Yuck!" he said, and stood up quickly.

"Mine's still nice," James said.

"You'll turn into a prune, James," Thomas said. "Time to get out."

James stood up as well, and Thomas tossed them both towels. Matthew's muscles rippled as he dried himself, while James's ribs showed, almost painfully.

"Ain't we heard the name Torrence before?" Matthew asked Thomas.

"Yes, we have."

"I don't remember it."

"You're too young," Thomas said. "We heard Pa tell Ma a story about a lawman who took money."

"Torrence?" James asked.

"That's the name."

"If he's a crooked lawman, why would Pa be friends with him?"

"He used to be friends with him," Matthew said. "He ain't no more."

"Then why talk to him?" the younger brother asked.

"He's the law here," Thomas said. "We got to see if the Langer gang has passed through here."

"If he's crooked, maybe he took money from them too," James said. "Maybe he'll lie."

"That's true," Thomas said, "but Pa knows that. Come on, get dressed. We got to meet Pa at the hotel."

"You think he's been talkin' to the sheriff all this time?" James asked.

"Probably not," Thomas said, pulling on his boots. "He's probably been walkin' around town tryin' to find out if the gang was here."

"And if the sheriff lied to him," Matthew said.

Thomas was the first to finish dressing, so he said, "I'll wait for you boys outside."

"What do you think Pa will do if he finds out the sheriff lied?" James asked.

"Whomp him," Matthew said, "or let me do it."

"Whomp the law?"

"Pa's the law," Matthew said,

"Not here, Matthew," James said, "and for sure not once we leave Texas." James pinned on his deputy's badge. "None of us will be."

Matthew pinned on his badge as well, and stood tall with it. "We're the law as long as Pa says we are."

James only nodded and pulled on his boots.

They joined Thomas outside the bath-house, and the three walked together toward the hotel. They saw their father standing in front, waiting for them.

"Has he talked to you, Thomas?" James asked.

"About Ma?"

"Yes."

"No," Thomas said. "He's keepin' it all inside."

"That can't be good," Matthew said.

"It's not gonna be good for the Langer gang when we catch up to them," Thomas said.

Shaye felt his chest swell with pride as his three sons walked toward him. They were washed and clean shaven, and though their clothes still bore the dirt of the trail, he knew their mother would have been proud as well.

He had intended to talked to them about the death of their mother, but found himself unable to do so. There was much to be done, and he wanted to hold onto his anger, his rage, until he caught up with Ethan Langer and his men. He was afraid that talking things out with his boys might drain that away, and he needed the full force of it to do what he had to do.

He stepped down off the boardwalk as his sons reached him. "I've never seen you boys looking so clean," he said. "Matthew, you're looking positively pink."

"You shoulda seen the water, Pa," Matthew said.

"James," Shaye said. "Clean shaven, I see."

"Yes, Pa."

"Well done," Shaye said. "I hope it itches less."

"Pa," Thomas said, "what did you find out from the sheriff?"

"What didn't I find out from the sheriff?" Shaye said. "Come on, I'll buy you boys a drink."

9

They walked to the nearest saloon — the
Lucky Ace — and Shaye told his sons about
his conversation with Sheriff Sam Torrence.

"You weren't exactly straight with us when
you said he was an old friend of yours, Pa,"
Thomas said.

"No, I wasn't, Thomas," Shaye said. "I
wasn't sure you boys would remember the
name."

"I didn't," James said. "Thomas and Matthew did."

"From a long time ago," Matthew said.

"Well, apparently Sheriff Torrence hasn't
changed much," Shaye said. "Fella at the
livery told me the Langer gang went through
here three days ago."

"Three days?" James said. "We're that
close?"

"We didn't ask," Matthew said, frowning.

"Well, I did," Shaye said. "I took my horse
in there right after you did, and I asked him.

I also paid him."

"You sure he was givin' you good information, Pa?" James asked.

"James, I trust his information more than I trust the sheriff's."

"What are we gonna do about the sheriff?" Thomas asked.

"Whomp 'im," Matthew said.

"Not quite, Matthew," Shaye said. "The sheriff still has time to tell us something."

"Like what?" James asked.

"Like what direction the Langer gang went."

"Ain't they goin' north?" Matthew asked. "I thought they was goin' north."

"We hope they're still going north," Shaye said. "Let's see what the sheriff tries to tell us."

"Why do you think he'll tell us anything?" James asked.

Shaye looked around. The saloon was pretty busy but they'd been able to secure a corner table. It didn't appear that anyone was paying attention to them.

"You think Langer left somebody behind?" Thomas asked.

"That's good thinking, Thomas," Shaye said. "Yeah, I was wondering if he might have left a man behind. Nobody seems to be paying us much mind, though."

Shaye was sitting so he could see the whole room. He gave his attention back to his sons.

"To answer your question, James," he said, "if the sheriff took money from Langer, it was to misdirect us. My guess is he'll come looking for me in a little while to do just that."

"And then we whomp 'im?" Matthew asked.

Shaye smiled at his middle son. "Be patient, Matthew," he said. "Maybe you'll get your chance."

Shaye made sure that he and his boys nursed only a beer or two, so that when Sheriff Sam Torrence came walking through the bat-wing doors, they would all be sober.

"Here he is," he said. "You boys take a walk over to the bar and let me talk to him."

Matthew and James stood up and obeyed immediately. Thomas hesitated.

"You sure you don't want me to stay, Pa?"

"I'll call you if I need you, Thomas. Don't worry."

Thomas cast a look Torrence's way, then turned and went to join his brothers at the bar.

Torrence walked over and joined Shaye at the table. "Three good-looking boys, Dan,"

50

he said, sitting down.

"Thanks."

"That big one looks just like you, only half again."

"The other two favor their ma."

"I can see that."

"You want a beer?"

"Not while I'm on duty, Dan," Sam Torrence said. "I'm makin' my rounds."

Shaye held back a laugh. "You come over here to tell me something, then?"

"I asked around," Torrence said. "Found out somethin' you should know."

"Like what?"

"Like the Langer gang is east of here."

"East? You sure?"

"That's what I heard."

"What would they be doing in New Mexico?"

"Checkin' out another bank?"

"No," Shaye said, "it's too soon. They have a pattern. Ethan hits a bank, Aaron hits a bank, and then they meet up."

"Maybe they're breakin' their pattern?"

"Not likely," Shaye said. "There's something else more likely."

"Like what?"

Shaye looked over at the bar and saw Thomas watching him. He nodded to his oldest son, who nudged his brothers. They

51

all came walking over.

"Sam, it's more likely you're lying to me," Shaye said.

Torrence looked up at the three young men standing around him, then back at Shaye. "Hey, Dan —"

"You're going to get up and walk out of here with us, Sam," Shaye said.

"Hey, hey, Dan —"

"If you make a fuss, I'll kill you."

Thomas and Matthew closed in on the lawman so he was in tight quarters. "And don't reach for your gun," Thomas said.

"You boys realize you're playin' with the law here?" Torrence asked, looking up at them.

"My pa's the law," Matthew said. "If he says to kill you, we'll kill you."

Torrence looked across the table at Shaye.

"What can I tell you, Sam?" he asked. "They're good boys." A steely look came over his face. "Get up."

10

They walked the sheriff out of the crowded saloon without anyone paying them any mind.

"Where to, Pa?" Thomas asked when they were outside.

"Let's go to his office," Shaye said. He prodded the lawman. "Lead the way."

Torrence led the four Shaye men to his office, which he unlocked.

"No deputies?" Shaye asked him.

"It's a quiet town."

They went inside.

"Lock the door, Thomas," Shaye said.

Matthew removed the sheriff's gun from his holster and shoved him across the room. The man staggered, banged his hip against his desk and righted himself.

"This ain't right, Dan," he said. "You got no jurisdiction, here."

"See these three boys?" Shaye asked. "They give me all the jurisdiction I need,

53

Sam. They'll do anything I tell them."

"You boys are gonna be in trouble if you keep doin' what your pa is tellin' you to do," Torrence warned.

Matthew turned and looked at Shaye. "Can I whomp 'im, Pa?"

"Go ahead, Matthew," Shaye said. "Whomp him good."

"Wha—" Torrence said, but Matthew took a step forward and smashed his fist into the man's face, cutting him off and knocking him back over the desk.

Torrence tried to get to his feet, a smear of blood across his face, as Matthew went around the desk to get him. Matthew hauled him back to his feet and hit him again, this time in the stomach, then straightened him up and hit him in the face again. The lawman went tumbling back and fell over his chair.

As Matthew bent over to pick him up again, Torrence yelled, "Dan, no more. Call 'im off!"

"Matthew," Shaye said.

But Matthew's own rage over the death of his mother had the blood roaring in his ears. He couldn't hear his father as he reached for Torrence and once again pulled him to his feet.

"Matthew!" Shaye shouted, but it did no

good. Matthew hit Torrence again, and then again.

"Boys!"

Thomas and James rushed forward to grab their brother's arms. They succeeded in pulling him off the lawman, who fell to the floor. Matthew was about to shrug them off when Shaye got in his face and shouted, "Matthew! That's enough!"

He stared at his father, swallowed hard, then said, "I whomped 'im, Pa."

"You sure did, Matthew," Shaye said. "You whomped him good. Let go of your brother, boys."

Thomas and James released Matthew, who stepped away from the fallen sheriff. Shaye turned and crouched over the fallen man, who was bleeding profusely now from cut lips and broken teeth.

"Sam? Can you hear me?"

"Uh —" Torrence said. "Juth keep him away. . . ." He wiped his mouth with his sleeve and stared down at the blood.

"Sam, which way did the Langer gang go?"

Torrence looked up at Shaye and tried to focus his eyes.

"Come on, Sam, stay with me," Shaye said. "Don't make me give you back to Matthew."

"Wha— Wha—"

"Which way did the Langer gang go?" Shaye asked again.

"N-North."

"Into Oklahoma Territory?"

Torrence nodded. "Yeth."

"They're not east of here?"

"No."

"That was a lie."

"Yeth."

Shaye straightened up and walked away from the man, away from the urge to kill him. Not only was he a disgrace to his badge, but he'd been trying to help the gang get away.

"Put him in his chair."

Thomas and James picked the sheriff up and did as they were told, then backed away. For a moment it looked like the local lawman would slide out of the chair again, but at the last minute he put his hands on his desk to steady himself.

Shaye kept his back turned for a few more moments until he had regained his composure, then turned and approached the desk. He leaned on it until his face was inches from Torrence's face.

"Two things, Sam. Are you listening?"

"Uh-huh."

"If we come back this way and you're still

wearing that badge, I'll kill you. Understand?"

"Uh, yeah . . ."

"And if I find out you tipped off Langer, sent him a telegram, whatever, I'll kill you. Got it?"

"I . . . got it. . . ."

Shaye turned and looked at his sons. "Get your horses, boys," he said. "We're leaving now."

11

The point of leaving Vernon immediately was so that Sheriff Torrence wouldn't get brave on them. They stopped and camped just outside of town, because Shaye didn't think Torrence would actually leave Vernon to chase them. He was crooked, he took money, but he wasn't a killer, and to keep his crookedness from the townspeople, he'd have to kill all four of them.

They ate a dinner of bacon and beans prepared by James and then Shaye said, "Thomas, James, why don't you go and check on the horses, and find more wood. I want to talk to your brother."

"Sure, Pa," Thomas said.

"Talk to him 'bout what?" James asked, but Thomas led him away from the fire.

"I know what you're gonna say, Pa," Matthew said before Shaye could begin to speak.

"And what's that, Matthew?"

"I got carried away when I was whompin'

the sheriff."

"Yes, you did."

"I just got so mad," Matthew said, balling his hands into fists and pressing them together, "thinkin' about him tryin' to help the gang get away from us."

"I know, Matthew," Shaye said. He reached across the fire and put his hand over his son's fists. "I was mad too. I wanted to kill him."

"You did?"

Shaye nodded.

"You didn't show it."

"I kept control of my emotions, Matthew," Shaye said. "That's not an easy thing to do."

Gently, Shaye was able to open his son's hands so they were no longer clenched tightly.

"But we have to try," he went on, "or our anger will get the better of us. It'll eat us up inside before we have a chance to finish what we started. Do you understand?"

"Yes, Pa."

"Your mother was very proud of you and your brothers," Shaye said, "of the men you had become. Let's not do anything that would shame her, okay?"

"Okay, Pa."

"Now, why don't you go and help your brothers."

"Yes, sir."

Shaye poured himself another cup of coffee as Matthew went off to find his brothers. His own anger had almost boiled over in the sheriff's office. He wondered if his sons would have had to pull him off of Sam Torrence if it hadn't been Matthew.

His boys probably didn't have any idea how tightly strung they were. Matthew had been the first to break, but he could see it in all three of them, just as he knew it was in himself. They were all like bowstrings that were about to snap, and it was his job to keep it from happening.

Perhaps the one thing he did not truly realize was just how close he actually was to breaking. With the responsibility of not only finding his wife's killers, but keeping his sons safe and in check, there was more and more pressure on him. A man who prided himself on his self-control, even he did not know what would happen when he finally lost it.

"What'd he want to talk to you about?" James asked Matthew while they searched for wood. Thomas had gone to check the horses, even though he knew his father had just given it to them as busy work.

"That's between me and Pa," Matthew said.

James straightened up, holding an armful of wood, and faced his brother. "It was about that whompin' you gave the sheriff, wasn't it? You woulda killed him if we hadn'ta stopped you."

"I was mad," Matthew said.

"I know," Jame replied. "I'm mad too. We all are. I hope Pa lets me whomp somebody before this is over."

"Little brother," Matthew said, "me and Thomas would have to hold somebody still for you to whomp 'em."

"You think so?" James stuck his jaw out belligerently. "I can handle myself, ya know."

"Yeah, James," Matthew said, "I know."

Thomas returned to the fire first and accepted the cup of coffee his father held out to him.

"You're the oldest, Thomas," Shaye said. "I need you to keep an eye on your brothers."

"I will, Pa."

"I swore on your mother's grave that I would try to keep you boys safe. Taking you along on this hunt was not the way to do that."

"We woulda followed you anyway."

"I figured as much."

They sat quietly for a few moments and then Thomas said, "Pa?"

"Yes?"

"Can I ask you somethin'?"

"Of course, Thomas."

"You ain't talked much about Ma. Don't you wanna talk about her?"

"I do, Thomas," Shaye said, "and I will. We'll talk a lot about her, but not until after this is all over. Is that all right?"

"Sure, Pa," Thomas said, "that's all right."

"Thank you, son."

12

Ethan Langer woke with a start, a scream sounding in his ears. It wasn't his own scream, for as he looked around the camp, no one was stirring or paying him any mind. He laid back down on his back and waited for his breathing to slow. It was that woman again, only hearing the scream was odd, because he recalled that when he'd run her down she hadn't made a sound.

Or had she?

Was he recalling her scream only in his dream?

No, he was sure she hadn't screamed at the time. The look on her face had been one of pure shock. She hadn't even had time to scream before she was trampled beneath his horse's hooves, and then those of the horses behind him.

Ethan wasn't sure why he kept dreaming about her. She was the first woman he'd ever killed, maybe that was it, but killing had never bothered him before. Why now? She hadn't been real young, but she had been pretty. He'd noticed her even before they hit the bank. She'd been across the street in the dress shop, but then he lost sight of her when they went into the bank. The next time he saw her, he was riding her down.

Someone stirred. He looked over and saw Petry at the fire, making a pot of coffee. He needed to get up and move around. He wished Aaron was there, but they were days, maybe weeks, from meeting up with his older brother. Besides, what could Aaron tell him? He'd probably make fun of him for dreaming about a woman he'd killed. Aaron had killed lots of people and, so far as he knew, not one of them haunted his dreams.

No, he couldn't tell Aaron about this, or anyone else for that matter. This was something he was going to have to deal with himself.

"Coffee's almost ready," Petry said to him when he approached the fire.

"Good."

"Sleep okay?"

"Fine," Ethan said. "Why would you ask me that?"

Petry shrugged and said, "I'm just makin'

64

conversation."

"Well, talk about somethin' else."

"You think we got a posse after us from Epitaph?"

"Why wouldn't we?" Ethan asked. "We robbed a bank. Don't they always send a posse after us when we do that? They won't cross into the territories, though. They got no jurisdiction."

"What about that woman we killed?"

"What about her?" Ethan snapped.

"Won't they cross the border 'cause of her?"

"Even if they do, they got no authority," Ethan said. "And if they catch up with us, we'll do what we always do."

"Take care of 'em?"

"That's right," Ethan said. "We'll take care of 'em."

Petry poured out a cup of coffee and handed it to his boss, who took it without thanks.

"I was just thinkin' about Epitaph — " he began, but Ethan cut him off.

"Jesus Christ, can't you talk about nothin' else?"

His voice was so loud he woke the rest of the camp. The men sat up or rolled out of their bedrolls and looked around to see what all the ruckus was about.

"It's time for all you sonsofbitches to get up!" Ethan shouted. "We got to get a move on."

"What about breakfast?" somebody asked.

"Fuck breakfast," Ethan said. "Have some coffee and get your damn horses saddled."

He stalked away from the fire with his coffee.

Red Hackett walked to the fire and took a cup of coffee from Terry Petry.

"What's eatin' him?" he asked, nodding toward Ethan.

"I don't know," Petry said. "He's been actin' real peculiar since we left Epitaph."

"Yeah, I noticed," Hackett said. "He ain't been sleepin' real good and he's real short-tempered."

"How can you tell?" Nick Taylor asked, coming up behind them. "He's always short-tempered, far as I can see."

"You ain't rode with him as long as we have," Petry said. "This is different."

"Well," Taylor said, "he killed that woman."

"We all killed her," Petry said. "We rode her down."

"Stupid bitch got in the way," Hackett said.

"Yeah, but Ethan's horse was the first one

to ride over her," Taylor said. "He killed her. He ever killed a woman before?"

Petry and Hackett exchanged a glance.

"Can't say I know," Hackett replied.

"Naw, that can't be it," Petry said. "Ethan's killed lots of people. Him and Aaron have killed more people than the rest of us put together."

"Yeah," Taylor said, reaching for some coffee, "but has he ever killed a woman? Makes a difference to some men."

Maybe, Terry Petry thought, but did it make a difference to Ethan Langer?

13

Ten days into the hunt, Shaye and his sons were in Oklahoma Territory. Their badges hadn't been much good since they'd left their own county, but now that they were in Oklahoma they were less than good.

"Should we even keep wearin' them, Pa?" James asked as they were about to cross the border.

"It can't hurt," Shaye said. "At the very least it'll get us some professional courtesy, even if we have no official standing."

Shaye knew they'd need all the professional courtesy they could get. Lawmen with vendettas were usually not looked upon very favorably by other lawmen, and Shaye had no illusions about his and his sons' motive for tracking the Langer gang. It was a vendetta, pure and simple — even though he'd had to explain to his boys just what "vendetta" meant.

"We won't speak of your mother's death

to these other lawmen we come across," Shaye told them. "In Oklahoma or anywhere else our hunt takes us."

"Why not, Pa?" Matthew had asked. "Won't they sympathize with us?"

"Professional lawmen remain objective, Matthew," Shaye had explained. "They don't let their emotions get in the way of doing their jobs."

"But you're a professional lawman, Pa," James said.

"We all are," Thomas said, "but I think what Pa is sayin' is that this is a special case."

"That's exactly right, Thomas," Shaye said. "It's special to us, but it's not going to be special to anyone else we run into. When we encounter other men with badges, we'll have to act like this is all in a day's work."

"But won't they know it's not?" Thomas asked. "After all, we're Texas lawmen in Oklahoma."

"We'll talk about the bank's money — the town's money — and the death of an innocent woman. We won't ever let them know who that woman was, though."

"I still don't get it —" Matthew began, but Thomas cut him off.

"This is the way Pa wants to do this, Matthew," he said. "He's the sheriff and we're his deputies. He knows what he's doin', so let's just do it his way, huh?"

"Well . . . okay." That explanation made sense to Matthew.

"James?" Thomas said.

"I understand what Pa is sayin', Thomas," James assured his older brother. "I'll go along with it."

"Good." Thomas had looked at his father then. "We're behind you, Pa."

"I know you are, boys," Shaye said, "and I appreciate it."

When they crossed into Oklahoma Territory, it was with a plan, and a new name for their hunt: "vendetta."

The first town they came to was called Lawton. If they continued due north, they would need to travel almost two hundred miles through Indian Territory before they came to Kansas. That was supposing the gang continued north and did not veer off and head in the direction of Oklahoma City.

They camped outside of Lawton, since there was no guarantee that Sam Torrence had indeed given up his badge and had not decided to spread the word that the Shaye men were wanted for assaulting a peace officer.

"You're part of a gang that has robbed a

70

bank and got away with a good amount of money," Shaye said to his sons. "Where would you go?"

"To a big town," Matthew said, "a city, and spend it."

"Like Oklahoma City?" Shaye asked.

"Yes."

"James?"

"I don't think I'd spend it right away, Pa," James said. "I wouldn't want anybody lookin' at me funny while I'm spending a lot of cash."

"That's good thinking, James," Shaye said, "but I'm afraid you're a little smarter than most bank robbers. How about you, Thomas?"

"Well," Thomas said, "if I'm Ethan Langer and I'm supposed to meet up with my older brother, Aaron, I don't think I'd spend a dime until I did — and I wouldn't let anyone else either."

"What about Oklahoma City?" Shaye asked.

"I wouldn't go there," Thomas said, "unless that's where I'm supposed to meet my brother."

"Well, with Aaron coming from South Dakota and Ethan from Texas, I think it's more likely they'd meet somewhere in Kansas."

"Kansas City?" Matthew asked, excited at the prospect.

"Too far east," Shaye said. "Wichita, maybe, or Salina."

"So we should head for Wichita?" James asked.

"If we guess Wichita and we're wrong," Thomas said, "we're settin' ourselves back, ain't we, Pa?"

"There's no time limit on revenge, Thomas," Shaye said. "But we won't commit to Wichita just yet. We got a long way to go, and there's bound to be more sightings of this gang. Ethan and Aaron Langer are well-known thieves. Somebody's going to spot them."

"And they won't lie to us the way Sam Torrence did, huh, Pa?" Matthew asked.

"Anybody who lies to us," Shaye said, "who tries to hinder us, Matthew, will have to deal with us. Time to turn in."

14

They rode into Lawton much the way they had ridden into Vernon — unshaven, unwashed, dirty. The horses were worn-out, and Shaye had decided they'd stay the night to give them — horses and men — a much-needed rest. He thought he might have been pushing them all too hard.

Lawton, Oklahoma, was a small but well-appointed-looking town. It seemed to be dragging itself toward the twentieth century, with streetlights and a trolley that went down the main street. There were some new brick and wood buildings, and the smell of newly cut lumber was in the air, a sure sign of a town that was growing.

They reined in their horses in front of a new-looking hotel called The Lawton House. To Shaye, it was a likely sign that a town was trying to improve itself when one of their hotels had the word "House" in the name — usually connected with the name of the town.

"Thomas, why don't you and James take the horses to the livery. Matthew and I will get us rooms, and then we'll go and find some good steaks."

"Sounds good, Pa."

Shaye and Matthew dismounted, removed their saddlebags and bedrolls, and handed over their horses. They were entering the hotel lobby as Thomas and James rode off, leading their horses.

"Good afternoon," the clerk said as Shaye and Matthew approached the front desk. "Welcome to Lawton, gentlemen. Can I get you a room?"

"Two, if you have them," Shaye said.

"Certainly." The clerk was in his thirties, well-dressed, short and slightly built, but with an air that said he was much more than just the desk clerk. "How long will you be staying with us?"

"Just overnight, more than likely," Shaye said.

The man turned the register around, and Shaye filled in the four names. He also took the opportunity to check the register to see if a bunch of men had checked in anytime in the past two weeks. He found nothing. When he turned the book back around, the man handed over two keys, to Rooms 3 and 4.

Shaye had decided that this time, in this town, they wouldn't ask about the Langer gang as loudly and obviously as they had during their very short stay in Vernon.

"We have a nice little town here," the clerk said. "You might decide to stay longer."

"Looks like your little town is growing," Shaye said, "but we're really just passing through."

"Well," the man said, "maybe next time, then."

"Are you the owner here?" Shaye asked.

"Yes, sir, I am."

"Do you have facilities with baths?"

"We certainly do," the man said. "In the back. How many shall I have drawn for you?"

"There are four of us. Can you accommodate that?"

"We have three tubs," the clerk said. "I'm sure you can work out the logistics between you."

"I think we can. Thank you."

"Will ten minutes do?"

"No," Shaye said. "I think we'll eat first. We're pretty hungry. Do you know where we can get a good steak?"

"Well, I do, but . . ."

"But what?"

"May I be candid?"

"Please."

"I really don't think you'd want to go into a restaurant looking — and smelling — like that."

Shaye looked at Matthew, then at himself, and said, "You might be right. Ten minutes will work, after all."

Shaye turned to Matthew and handed him the key to Room 4. "Wait for your brothers outside and give them the key."

"Yes, Pa. . . . Pa?"

"Yes, Matthew?"

"We got to take baths again?"

"Yes, Matthew," Shaye said, "we have to take baths again."

Thomas and James dismounted and walked all four horses into the livery. The liveryman turned and smiled at them. He was tall and older, in his sixties, and was wiping his gnarled hands on a rag as they entered.

"Help you gents?"

"We'd like to put our horses up for the night, have them rubbed down and fed," Thomas said.

"I take good care of animals I take into my charge," the man said, "yes sir."

"That's good," James said. "They need

some care."

The man looked the animals over critically. "Been riding them hard and long, looks like."

"Some," Thomas said.

"Well, I'll give them care and a good night's rest. How long you plannin' on leavin' them with me?"

"Just overnight," Thomas said.

"Good enough," the man said with a nod. "They'll be ready to go in the mornin'."

"Much obliged," Thomas said.

"Lawmen, I see," the man commented, noticing the badges on their shirts.

"That's right," Thomas said, "from Texas."

"A little far from home, ain'tcha?"

"We're just passin' through," Thomas said, remembering his father's warning not to ask questions.

"Lookin' fer somebody, are ya?"

"My brother said we're just passin' through," James answered.

"Sure, sure," the man said. "Well, my name's Ike. I guess I'll be seein' you boys in the mornin'."

"What do we owe you?" Thomas asked.

"You kin pay me in the mornin'," Ike said. "If I can't trust the law, who can I trust, right?"

"Thanks," James said.

He and Thomas recovered the saddlebags and bedrolls from their saddles, bid Ike good afternoon, and left the livery.

"Too many questions for my taste," James commented as they left.

"I was thinkin' the same thing, little brother."

When they reached the hotel, they found Matthew waiting for them with a key.

"You bunkin' with Pa tonight?" Thomas asked, accepting the key.

"I guess," Matthew said with a shrug. "He didn't say."

"Might as well," Thomas said. "You checked in with him."

"We got to take baths," Matthew said. "Pa says so."

"Before we eat?" James asked.

"The hotel clerk said we smelled."

"You do smell," Thomas said.

"So do you," Matthew said.

"I didn't say I didn't," Thomas replied, "I just said you did."

"You think I smell worse than you?"

"You're bigger," James said. "There's more of you to smell. You smell worse than me 'n' Thomas put together."

Matthew lifted an arm and sniffed himself carefully. "I smell fine."

"Well," Thomas said, "all I know is, I ain't usin' the same tub as you unless I go before you."

"Man said he got three tubs."

"As long as I get to one before you fill it with mud," Thomas said.

Thomas and James walked past their brother, who took one more sniff of himself before following them.

15

When they reached the restaurant called Magnolia's, Shaye could see why the clerk had warned him about bathing first. It looked like a family place, with couples as well as people with children dining. Everyone was dressed better than they were. They had donned extra clothes they'd brought with them, but they were still trail clothes, though at least they were clean.

"Gentlemen," a man in a dark suit said, fronting them, "a table for four?"

"Please," Shaye said.

"This is fancy, Pa," Matthew said, clearly uncomfortable.

"Don't worry, Matthew," Shaye said, "the food will be fine."

"People are lookin' at us."

"They're lookin' at you," James said, poking Matthew from behind. "You have your hair parted in the middle."

"Leave your brother alone, James," Shaye

said. "They're looking at our badges."

They were led to their table, where they were seated between a middle-aged couple and a family of three, with a little girl.

"A waiter will be right with you," the man said, and left.

"I thought he was our waiter," Matthew said.

"His job is to show us to our table," James said.

"Why couldn't he take our order?" Matthew asked. "It don't seem so hard."

"It's not his job, Matthew," Thomas said.

"We're all having steaks and beer, right?" Shaye asked.

His three sons agreed.

"Some people are still lookin' at us, Pa," James said.

"They're curious why four lawmen are in here," Shaye said. "Don't worry about it. Word will probably get to the local law and he'll come looking for us with some questions."

"What are you gonna tell him?" Thomas asked.

"I'll see what the questions will be before I decide that," Shaye said, "but remember one thing — I'll do the talking. Okay?"

They agreed.

When a waiter appeared, Shaye ordered

four steak dinners and four beers. Matthew looked over at the little blond girl at the next table and smiled at her. Her mother leaned over, hissed at her and made her turn away.

"Scarin' little girls again?" James whispered to his brother.

Matthew just scowled at him.

Their steaks came and Shaye ate while watching and listening to his boys. Shaye rarely interfered when his sons were arguing or kidding with each other. Mary had always said the boys should work things out for themselves. The only time she ever interfered or had him interfere was when they came to blows — which they did often as small boys but hardly ever as young adults.

Thomas was very smart, but James had the quickest mind. Shaye knew that Matthew probably had the softest heart and was an easy target for both of his brothers if they wanted to pick on him. He was physically intimidating, but would never lay a hand on either of them in anger.

And all three boys cleaned up very well, and Shaye knew that girls liked them. Thomas was very good with women, Matthew too shy, and James was learning by watching his older brother. Shaye knew they all got their personalities from their mother, because he kept to himself most of the time and, except for Mary, didn't like other people very much.

By the time they finished their dinners, the people at the tables surrounding them had changed, but they were still pretty much the center of attention. They all ordered pie and coffee and were almost finished with that when a man with a badge entered the restaurant. He stood just inside the door, easily located them, and started toward their table.

"Here comes the local law, boys," Shaye said. "Remember, I'll do all the talking."

The boys nodded as the lawman approached.

16

"Gentlemen," the sheriff said when he reached their table, "my name's Ray Stover. I'm the sheriff here in Lawton."

"Sheriff," Shaye said. The man was his age and had the look of a longtime lawman. "Pleased to meet you. I'm Dan Shaye, sheriff of Epitaph, Texas. These are my sons, and my deputies."

"Shaye?"

"That's right."

"I've heard of you."

"Have you?"

"You been in Texas a long time, haven't you?"

"Twelve years or so."

"I heard of you before that, though."

"Maybe you did."

Stover licked his lips. "If you boys wouldn't mind comin' to my office when you're done eatin'," he said, "we could talk there."

"I reckon I could come on over, Sheriff," Shaye said, "although I don't see any reason for the boys to come with me, do you?"

"I suppose not," Stover said.

"Good," Shaye said. "I'll come over in a little while and we'll have a talk."

"That's fine," Stover said. "Uh, enjoy your meals."

"Thanks, Sheriff."

Folks in the restaurant watched as Ray Stover left the place, then focused their attention back on Shaye and his sons.

"What was that about, Pa?" Thomas asked.

"What did he mean, he heard of you?" James asked.

"Can we get some more pie?" Matthew asked.

"You can have some more pie, Matthew," Shaye said. "I'm going to have to go and talk with the sheriff for a while, boys. When I'm done, I'll come to the hotel and we can talk some."

"About what?" James asked.

"About your questions," Shaye said. He took the napkin off his lap and dropped it on the table. "Thomas, you got enough money to pay for dinner?"

"Yes, Pa."

"Then get your brother some more pie,"

he said, standing, "pay for dinner, and I'll see you all back at the hotel. Maybe we'll go and have another beer and talk."

"Sure, Pa," Thomas said.

All three boys watched their father leave the restaurant, as did the other patrons.

"What do you think that's about, Thomas?"

"I don't know, James," Thomas said, "but I guess we'll find out soon enough."

17

Shaye knocked on the lawman's door before he entered, out of courtesy. Ray Stover was seated behind his desk and watched nervously as Shaye closed the door behind him.

"Coffee?" Stover asked, holding up a mug of his own.

"No, thanks," Shaye said. "I had enough over at the restaurant." He sat in a chair opposite the local lawman. "Pretty nice place for a small town."

"We're growin'," Stover said.

"I can see that."

The two men studied each other for a few moments. Stover took a sip from his mug, and Shaye had a feeling the contents was not coffee.

"You're Shaye Daniels, aren't you?" Stover finally asked. "*The* Shaye Daniels?"

"I'm Sheriff Dan Shaye these days, Sheriff," Shaye said. "What's past is past."

"I thought you was dead."

"Not dead," Shaye said. "Just living in South Texas."

"And wearin' a badge."

"That's right."

"Well . . . who woulda thought it?"

"Not me," Shaye said, "not fifteen years ago, anyway."

"So what are you doin' in Oklahoma?" he asked.

"We're passing through, actually."

"Not lookin' for anyone in particular?"

"Like who?"

Stover shrugged. "I heard somethin' about a bank robbery in South Texas, thought maybe that had somethin' to do with you bein' here."

"Bank robbery," Shaye said, frowning. "You think a bank robbery would bring me this far from home, Sheriff?"

"I don't know," Stover said. "I heard it was the Langer gang."

"What else did you hear?'

"That they also hit a bank in South Dakota."

"The Langers."

"That's right."

"Ethan and Aaron, right?"

"Right."

"You know either one of them, Ray?"

"Uh, no, not really."

"What's that mean, not really, Ray?"

"I mean, I may have met Ethan a time or two, but we ain't, uh, friends, or anything."

"Then what are you?"

"Well . . ." Stover moved his shoulders nervously. He looked into his cup, and apparently it was empty. He licked his lips.

"Go ahead, Ray," Shaye said. "Have another drink. You don't mind if I call you Ray, do you?"

"Uh, no, not at all," the lawman said. He took a bottle of whiskey from the bottom drawer of his desk and poured a generous dollop into his mug. He put the bottle back, then sipped gingerly from the mug.

"Does Ethan call you Ray?"

"Huh? Uh, no."

"What's he call you?"

Stover shifted uncomfortably. "I ain't seen Ethan Langer in years."

"He hasn't passed through here recently?"

"You're after him, ain'tcha?"

"I told you, Sheriff," Shaye said, "we're just passing through. However, if I happened to run into the Langer gang, I'd count it my duty to bring them in. Wouldn't you?"

"I sure would."

"Then I guess they haven't passed through here."

"If they came this way," Stover said, "they by-passed comin' into town."

"Well, lucky for them," Shaye said, "or for you." He stood up. "How long you been sheriff here?"

"A few years."

"What'd you do before that?"

"Wore a badge some other places."

"So you never rode with the Langers, or anything like that."

"No," Stover said, "I never did."

"Yeah," Shaye said, "I had you figured for a longtime lawman. You like it here?"

"I like it fine," Stover said. "It's a growin' town. I wouldn't wanna do anythin' to mess up this job."

"Well, I hope you don't," Shaye said. "I hope you hold onto this job for a long time to come."

"Uh, thanks."

"Enjoy your drink."

Stover looked into his cup, then set it aside. "I reckon I had enough."

"We'll be moving on tomorrow, Sheriff," Shaye said. "We just stopped overnight for some rest."

"That's fine," Stover said. "That's just fine."

Shaye walked to the door and stepped outside without a word. Sheriff Ray Stover had recognized all of the names involved — his, Ethan and Aaron Langer's — but Shaye doubted he knew more than that. The man was too comfortable in his job to want to mess it up, just like he said.

As he walked toward the hotel, he wondered just how much he was going to have to tell his sons.

18

The boys were waiting for him outside the hotel. Thomas and James had found chairs, and Matthew was leaning against a pole.

"You boys could have waited inside."

"What's goin' on, Pa?" Thomas asked.

Shaye looked up and down the street, spotted a saloon several doors down. It was open, looked and sounded quiet. It'd be dark soon, and the saloon wouldn't be quiet for long.

"Let's get a beer, boys," Shaye said. "I think there's some things about your pa you should know."

When they got settled at a table in the Aces Up saloon, each with a beer in front of them, Dan Shaye told his boys a story about a young outlaw named Shay Daniels. . . .

When he was sixteen years old, Danny Shaye's parents both died of a mysterious fever that made it necessary for all of their belongings — and their Missouri home — to be burned afterward. Too old to be adopted, too ornery and bitter to live with anyone else, Danny was left to fend for himself. He decided to do it with a gun, using the name "Shay Daniels."

Practicing until he was proficient and deadly with his father's Colt, he proceeded to terrorize most of Missouri and Kansas, and some of Oklahoma Territory. By the time he met Mary Fitzgerald and married her, when he was in his late and she in her early twenties, he had earned a full-fledged reputation as an outlaw and gunman, and was wanted in three states. He continued to try to live in Missouri, Kansas, or Oklahoma, but finally tired of having to sneak home to see Mary and their three boys.

Finally, he decided to take the family and move to Texas, where he was not wanted at all, or even that well known. He heard about a South Texas town called Epitaph that was looking to hire a sheriff — not run one for election, but hire one. He applied for the job, got it, and moved his family there. In his late thirties he became Sheriff "Dan" Shaye, and left Shay Daniels in the past.

Until now . . .

■ ■ ■ ■

That's the story Shaye told his three sons, figuring they didn't need to hear the whole story.

"You were an outlaw?" Matthew asked, eyes wide.

"A gunman?" James asked.

"I remember," Thomas said. "I remember, as a kid, wondering why you were away so much."

"Now you know," Shaye said. He looked at Matthew and James. "I was never as bad as my reputation made me out to be — but that's how reputations go."

"How many men did you kill?" James asked.

"That's not important, James," Shaye said.

"The reason I'm telling you this is that now that we're out of Texas and in Oklahoma — and we'll probably be going to Kansas as well — there's bound to be others who will remember the old Danny Shaye."

"Is that why you hardly ever left Texas before?" Thomas asked. "Except to go to Ol' Mexico, or Louisiana, or New Mexico? Never north?"

"That's why, Thomas," Shaye said. "I just

never wanted to have to deal with the old stories."

"Is that why this sheriff was scared of you?" Matthew asked. "Because of your reputation?"

"I suppose so," Shaye said. "He's just the right age to remember what I used to be."

"I'm having a hard time understanding this," James said. "Why don't I remember any of this?"

Shaye looked at his youngest son.

"You were only seven when we moved to Texas, James," he said. "There's no reason why you should remember." He looked at all three of his sons. "There's no reason why any of you should remember anything. Your mother and I kept it from you."

"Why would Ma marry an outlaw?" Matthew asked.

All three of the other men looked at him.

"What kind of a question is that?" Thomas asked.

"It's a fair question, Thomas," Shaye said. "Your mother was a wonderful woman. She saw things in me I didn't even know existed. She got me off that path, but by that time no one in Missouri or Kansas or Oklahoma would give me a chance. That was why we had to move to Texas to start over."

"And they made you sheriff of Epitaph

even though you were an outlaw?" Matthew asked.

"Nobody in South Texas knew my name," Shaye said. "They accepted me for what I showed them, and they liked that I had brought a family with me. They figured that meant I'd settle down and keep the job for a long time."

"Twelve years," Thomas said. "That is a long time."

"I want you boys to understand this doesn't change who I am," Shaye said. "I'm still your father, the same man you've always known. I'm still me."

All three boys studied him, and he knew it couldn't be helped. He looked different in their eyes at that moment, but he hoped they'd be able to adjust.

"What happened with the sheriff, Pa?" Thomas asked. Shaye was grateful to his older son for having the presence of mind to change the subject.

Shaye told them about his meeting with the lawman, who knew not only his reputation but that of the Langer brothers as well.

"Do you think he'll let them know we're lookin' for them?" Thomas asked.

"I don't think he'll do anything to jeopardize his position here," Shaye said. "He likes it here too much."

"So he can't help us," James said.

"No."

"So what do we do now?" Matthew asked.

"We get a good night's sleep," Shaye said, "and in the morning we keep heading north." He hesitated, then added, "That is, unless one or two or all of you want to head back."

The three boys exchanged a glance, and then Thomas said, "We're goin' where you go, Pa."

"Well, good," Shaye said, "because right now I'm going to my hotel room to get some rest."

19

Of course, turning in early did not appeal to Thomas, Matthew, and James, so while Shaye went to his room to rest, they went in search of a saloon.

"Stay out of trouble," was all their father told them. "Thomas, I'll hold you responsible for your brothers' actions, as well as your own."

"Yes, Pa."

They found a small saloon, not crowded, no gaming tables, and two girls working the floor. When they entered, the girls noticed them immediately and joined them by the time they reached the bar.

"I'm Dora," one said. She was blond and pretty.

"I'm Henri," the other, a small brunette, said.

"Henri?" Matthew asked.

"Short for Henrietta." She pressed herself up again him. "You're big. I like big men."

"And you two are cute," Dora said to Thomas and James. "You kinda look alike."

"We're brothers," James said. "All three of us."

"Ooh," Henri said, touching Matthew's badge, "and lawman. How exciting."

"Where is . . . Epi-tat?" Dora asked, peering intently at Thomas's badge.

"It's in South Texas."

"Well," she said, holding onto his arm, "you're a long way from home, Sheriff."

"We're deputies," Matthew said.

"Deputies or sheriffs," Dora said, "you probably need some company."

Since the saloon was empty, the girls were able to spend a lot of time with them, flattering them and getting them to buy two or three beers instead of just one and nursing it. Still, Thomas was mindful of his father's warning that he would be held responsible for any shenanigans, so he left it to his brothers to flirt with the girls while he watched for trouble. After all, most of the fights he'd been in up to now in his young life had been over a girl. And these two were just pretty enough and smart enough to cause a big one. However, as long as the saloon was empty . . .

The Shaye boys had been in the saloon

about an hour when the bat-wing doors opened and some regulars arrived. Of the six who entered, two of them — Pat Booth and Tim Daly — considered Dora and Henri to be their girls. It didn't matter how many times the girls told them they were "working" girls, when Pat and Tim entered the saloon with their friends in tow, they expected to be fawned over.

"What the hell!" Pat said, touching Tom on the arm. "What are those three jaspers doin' with our women?"

"I don't know," Tim said.

From behind, their four friends — all from the same ranch — nudged them, and one of them said, "Looks like your ladies got themselves some new beaus."

"Yeah, well not for long," Tim said, and marched over to where Dora and Henri were entertaining the Shayes. Pat followed him, and the others trailed along.

"What are you strangers doin' with our women?" Pat demanded.

Matthew and James turned to face the men, who caught sight of the stars on their chest.

Pat got a nudge from behind and somebody whispered in his ear, "Lawmen."

The six were just ranch hands, and the only laws they broke was when they got into a fight in some saloon each week and caused some damage.

Pat grabbed for Tim's arm, but Tim pulled it away.

"They're lawmen, Tim," Pat said hastily.

"That don't make no never mind," Tim said, peering at their badges. "They ain't local. They got no — watchacallit — jurisprudence here."

"Hey, friend," Thomas said, "we were just keepin' the ladies company until you got here. Why don't we all have a drink and you can take your girls with you —"

"We ain't their girls!" Dora complained loudly.

"Yeah," Henri agreed, holding tightly to Matthew's thick arm. "They think we are, but we're always telllin' them we're not." She looked up at Matthew, fluttered her eyelashes at him and said, "Make them go away, Matthew . . . please?"

"Matthew —" Thomas said, but he was too late.

The larger of the three brothers turned to face the ranch hands full on and said, "You heard the ladies, gents. Move along."

"James," Thomas said, but his young brother had already turned to face the six men so he could back up Matthew.

"You hear that, Pat?" Tim asked. "Now

they're sayin' they ain't our girls."

"Well," Pat said, "maybe they ain't, Tim —"

"Pat's givin' his girl away, now," Lou, one of the other men, said. He was big and beefy, and nudged Pat so hard that he propelled him forward, almost into Matthew, who put his big hand out to steady him.

"Easy," Matthew said.

"Don't push!" Pat snapped. He was talking to Lou, but Matthew thought he was talking to him.

"I didn't push you, friend," he said. "I just put out my hand to keep you from fallin', is all."

"No, I didn't mean —" Pat started, but Tim pulled him out of the way so he could face Matthew, who now became his focus.

"You think your badge scares me?" he demanded. "Or your size? My pal Lou, here, could eat you for breakfast."

Matthew looked at Lou, who puffed out his chest and smiled. Lou Scales was in his thirties, a full ten or twelve years older than Matthew. He was roughly the same height, but clearly out-weighed the younger man by thirty pounds or more — most of it around his middle.

"My brother could handle your friend

with no problem," James shot back.

Thomas could see the situation getting out of hand. It had switched from the girls to who was bigger or badder, Matthew or this fella Lou.

"Now look, fellas," he said, "nobody wants any trouble —"

"Your badges don't mean nothin' here!" Tim snapped.

"You're right about that," Thomas said, still trying to defuse the situation.

"We could kick the crap out of the three of you and nobody could do anything about it."

"Well," Thomas said, "that's not quite true. I mean, we'd have to try and do somethin' about it —"

"Me and my brothers can handle six saddle tramps like you!" James spat.

"Oh yeah?" Tim asked.

Thomas knew he couldn't be sucked into this, that he had to do something before somebody went for a gun. They had become the center of attention in the saloon, which had suddenly become crowded. Now, as if sensing that gunplay was in the offing, everyone shrank away from them, hugging the walls and giving them room.

In that single moment the action could have gone in many directions.

20

Thomas was wracking his brain, trying to find a way to avoid trouble, when James spoke up.

"You know," the younger brother said, "this really wouldn't be fair, six against three. We got enough witnesses here who would say it wasn't a fair fight."

That seemed to stop Tim and his friends for a moment.

"My brother's right," Thomas said. "There's a way to resolve this without anybody gettin' in trouble, or gettin' hurt."

"Resolve?" Tim asked, frowning.

"Settle it," Thomas said, "there's a way to settle this."

The six ranch hands seemed to need a way to settle it, since Thomas had already offered them the girls.

"Howzat?" Tim asked.

Tim looked at James to see if he had anything to say, but the younger brother simply shrugged. It was up to Thomas to come up with a clever solution.

Since Matthew and Lou were still eyeing each other, Thomas said, "We each pick one man, and the two of them go at it."

Tim frowned. "Go at it how? Guns?"

"No," Thomas said, "no guns. I don't think the situation calls for guns, do you? After all, somebody could end up getting killed, and over what? A couple of girls?"

"Hey!" Dora said, but the men ignored her.

"Well," Tim said, "maybe not . . ."

"Knives?" one of the other ranch hands offered.

"Somebody still gets hurt, or killed," James said.

"Or arrested," Thomas said.

"A fight, then," Tim said. "Our big man against yours."

Thomas looked at Matthew, who was still exchanging hostile glances with Lou. He remembered what had happened when his brother started to whomp the sheriff in Vernon. Getting into a barfight would constitute getting into trouble as far as Dan Shaye was concerned, and he would be held responsible.

"Arm wrestling!" James suddenly said.

"What?" Tim asked.

"That's a good idea," Thomas said. "We'll have an arm wrestling match. My brother Matthew against your man Lou." Thomas slapped his brother on the back.

"What are the stakes?" Tim asked.

"The winners get the girls," Thomas said.

"And the losers have to buy the drinks," James added.

"That suits me," Matthew said.

Tim turned and looked at his companions. Pat shrugged and looked over at Lou.

"Suits me too," Lou said. "This fella's nothin'."

"Let's get a table ready!" James shouted.

Some of the other patrons, now that they knew there was to be no gunplay, got involved. They brought over a table and two chairs, and Thomas pulled both of his brothers aside.

"Matthew, can you take this guy?" he asked. "He's got that belly, and that'll anchor him."

"It don't matter, Thomas," Matthew assured his older brother. "I'll break him down. I ain't never been beat in arm wrestling."

"I know," Thomas said, "in Epitaph. But this fella's older, and he's heavier."

"It don't matter, I tell ya."

Thomas looked at James.

"I think we should take bets," James said. "What do you think?"

"That's what I was thinkin'," Thomas said, "as long as Matthew is sure."

"I been lookin' into his eyes," Matthew told them. "I can beat 'im."

"James?" Thomas said.

"I'm on it."

Suddenly, it turned into a betting match, and James was moving all around the room taking action. Tim, on the other side, seeing that, started doing the same thing.

The two participants, Matthew and Lou Scales, stood facing each other on either side of the table. Neither would sit until the match was about to start.

"Wait a minute!" Tim called out.

"What is it?" Thomas asked.

"We need a referee."

"Somebody impartial," James said.

The brothers knew they were at a disadvantage since they didn't know anybody in the saloon, and the ranch hands were local.

"It don't matter," Matthew said to Thomas and James. "We ain't gonna need a referee to decide the winner."

"No," Lou Scales said, "we ain't, because I'm gonna tear this pup's arm off."

"Then the bartender will do," Thomas said. "Any objections?"

Nobody objected. Probably the most impartial person in any saloon was the bartender anyway.

"Okay, then," James said, "we might as well get started."

21

Alone in his room, Dan Shaye realized that being alone was not a good thing for him. All he did was think about his dead wife. That fueled his anger and his bitterness, and without an outlet, they could combine to eat him alive from the inside out. He decided to go see what the boys were up to. He was fairly certain Thomas could keep them out of trouble, but there was no harm in checking.

The two men seated at the table were the center of attention. All the others — all men except for the two saloon girls — crowded around them. Some climbed on top of tables to see, others stood on the bar. Most of the people in the place had a monetary interest in the outcome.

Thomas watched the action with satisfaction. A potentially dangerous situation had become a sporting event, and that was much preferred.

He hoped his father would feel the same way, because at that moment he saw Dan Shaye walk into the saloon.

From the street, Shaye had noticed all the commotion coming out of the small saloon, and he walked over hoping he would not find his sons in there. As soon as he entered, though, he knew he was out of luck. He could feel their presence.

He pushed his way through the crowd until he saw Matthew sitting at a table across from a man who was as big as a bull. Then he saw Thomas, on the other side of the table, looking at him. He hadn't seen James yet, so he circled his way to his oldest son.

"Hello, Pa," Thomas said.

"Thomas," Shaye said. "Do we have any money on this little contest?"

"Uh, some."

"Where's James?"

"He's right over there." Shaye looked where Thomas was pointing and saw his youngest son standing among a bunch of bar patrons.

"And why are we here?"

"It was either this or a bar fight," Thomas said, "or worse."

"And what started it?"

"Uh, that big guy and five of his friends."

"Over what?"

"Well . . ."

"Girls?"

"Yup."

"Those two standing on the bar?"

Thomas turned and saw that a couple of men had helped Dora and Henri up onto the bar so they could see better.

"I'm afraid so," Thomas said. "They came up to us, Pa. I swear, the place was empty when we got here, but —"

"Save it, Thomas," Shaye said. "Looks like they're about to start. That big guy looks like he's going to be tough. Big belly on him. It'll anchor him."

"That's what I thought, Pa," Thomas said, "but Matthew said he could take him."

"I guess we're about to find out if he's right."

22

Dan Shaye watched as his son Matthew dug his feet into the floor. He thought he could actually see the muscles of his tree-stump-like legs tensing. Matthew was going to try to use the strength of his legs to counteract the bigger man's heavy center. If he was able to do that, it would come down to the man with the most arm strength.

The bartender got the two men to clasp hands, held them steady with his own hands, then released them and said, "Go."

Immediately, the place erupted in shouting, yelling, and whistling as the men — and the two ladies — rooted for the man they had their money on.

"If your brother wins," Shaye said into Thomas's ear, "are his partners going to go along with it?"

"They should," Thomas said. "It's only gonna cost them the two girls, and drinks."

Shaye turned and looked at the two cute

saloon girls on the bar. They were jumping up and down, waving their arms, their breasts bouncing so much they were threatening to take some of the attention away from the contest in the center of the floor.

"Go!" the bartender said, but neither man moved.

Well, in fact it only looked as if neither man moved. Actuality, they were pushing against each other, and neither was making any headway.

"This could be a battle of attrition," Shaye said in Thomas's ear.

"What?"

"One of them will have to wear the other one down."

"Oh," Thomas said, nodding.

One of Mary's concerns about moving to South Texas had been that the boys would not receive a proper education. She had attended college in the East. Shaye had gone as far as the eleventh grade in St. Louis until he went out on his own. Both were considered better educated than the average westerner. The boys had ended up in a one-room schoolhouse in Epitaph, and had also received some tutoring at home from their mother.

Watching Matthew, he admired how, in profile, his middle son seemed to resemble

113

a Greek god. While he did not consider Matthew simple-minded, the boy did have a rather simple outlook on life. He concentrated on one thing at a time, whether it was eating a piece of pie or arm wrestling. At that moment his face was a mask of concentration, and Shaye suddenly knew that Matthew was going to win. The other man's eyes were already moving around, unable to hold Matthew's, and his legs were beginning to tremble. For a big man, he did not have very thick legs, and his belly was not giving him the advantage it might have.

Now Matthew was bringing the man's arm down toward the table, slowly but surely. The crowd got into it, screaming and shouting louder, while Shaye, Thomas, and James watched silently. The look on Lou Scales's face was panicky as he too realized he was on the verge of losing.

Abruptly, Scales changed his tactic. He stood up and pulled Matthew across the table toward him. He intended to smash Matthew in the face with his fist, but Matthew was too fast for him. He blocked the blow and sent the bigger man staggering back.

"The youngster wins!" the bartender shouted, but a backhanded blow from Lou

Scales sent him staggering back against the bar.

Embarrassed, Lou Scales was furious, and he tossed away the table that was between himself and Matthew.

"Pa?" Thomas asked.

"Let it go, Thomas," Shaye said. "Matthew has to finish this now. Where are the other man's friends?"

"Grouped over there," Thomas said, pointing.

"All right," Shaye said, locating them. "Any one of them goes for his gun, you kill him. You understand?"

"Yes, Pa."

"Don't hesitate, Thomas," Shaye said, "or your brother will pay the price."

"Yes, sir."

The once explosive, once defused, situation had become explosive again.

23

Shaye watched as Matthew squared off against the larger, older man. He stood his ground and wasn't about to back down. Whatever the original reason had been for the dispute — girls, drinks — it now appeared to be the older man's embarrassment at having been bested in arm wrestling. Whether this was a good enough reason for his companions to go for their guns remained to be seen.

Shaye looked over at his youngest son, and James seemed to be in his element. He was now taking bets on who would win the fight, while Shaye would have preferred that he watch his brother's back. He knew he would have to talk to James about his priorities when this was all over.

The two big men in the center of the room came together then. They grappled, and just when it looked as if they were going to wrestle, the older man unleashed a punish-

ing right that hit Matthew in the belly.
Matthew's entire body seemed to shudder
— and so did Shaye's, as if he could feel his
son's pain — but the younger man did not
back up. Instead he set his legs and launched
a punch of his own, which landed on Lou
Scales's jaw. Scales had apparently expected
Matthew to go down from the body blow,
and as a result had left himself open for a
counterpunch. His head rocked back, and
before he could recover, Matthew moved in
and threw a body punch of his own. Scales's
girth, which might have benefited him during the arm wrestling match if he'd used it
correctly, was now of no use to him at all.
His soft belly absorbed Matthew's punch,
and as all the air was crushed from his
lungs, his eyes went wide and his face grew
red. Matthew did not wait to see the re-
sponse from his blow. He stepped back,
measured the man, and hit him with a
thunderous uppercut that rocked Scales's
head back, straightened him up, then sent
him toppling backward until he slammed
into the floor on his back. His leg twitched
for a moment, and then he lay completely
still.

Shocked to see Scales beaten by three
punches, his friends were unsure what to
do. They looked to Tim Daly and Pat Booth,

who were their leaders, but they were as unsure as the rest. Watching them, Shaye knew they were going to make the wrong decision.

As their hands drifted to their guns he stepped forward and said, "Don't even think about it!"

Suddenly, he was the center of attention. James turned away from the men he'd been collecting money from and looked at his father. Thomas stepped forward to stand with his father and Matthew. A moment later James joined them.

The ranch hands saw that their six to three advantage had now turned into five against four. They did not like the odds at all.

"It's all over, boys," Shaye said. "Pick up your friend and take him home. There's no point in anyone getting seriously hurt over this."

"Uh, Pa . . ." James said.

Shaye looked at his younger son, then said to the ranch hands, "Pay off your debts and then take your friend home."

The five men were still unsure what to do, but another man had now entered the room, wearing a local badge rather than the Texas ones the Shayes were wearing.

"What's goin' on?" he demanded.

Dozens of men started talking at the same

time, but Sheriff Stover spotted Shaye and his sons and walked over to them.

"Just a little misunderstanding, Sheriff, between my sons and some of your local hands," Shaye said. "It turned into an arm wrestling match, and then a fight."

Stover looked down at the fallen man and raised his eyebrows. Then he looked up at Matthew. "Your son put Lou Scales down?"

"With three punches!" James said proudly. "He beat him in arm wrestling, and then in the fight."

Stover noticed the handful of money James was holding. "And there was betting goin' on?"

"Just some friendly wagers, Sheriff," Shaye said. "That's not against the law, is it?"

Stover didn't answer. Instead he looked over at Daly, Booth, and the others. "You boys better pay off your bets and get Lou out of here," he said. "The rest of you go back to whatever you were doin'."

Dora and Henri came running over to press themselves against James and Matthew.

"I might have figured you two were involved in this," Stover said. "Always teasing those ranch hands."

"It was Daly and them who started it,

Sheriff," the bartender said. "These three was just havin' a drink and talkin' to the girls."

"Okay, thanks, Harve," Stover said. "You might as well get back behind the bar."

There was a lot of movement, shuffling of feet, shifting of tables and chairs, until the room looked almost back to normal.

"You boys figure on stickin' around the saloon awhile?" Stover asked the three Shaye boys.

"They were just going to turn in for the night, Sheriff," Shaye said. "Weren't you, boys?"

"That's right, Pa," Thomas said.

"Yeah," Dora said, "with us!"

"No, ladies," Shaye said, "I'm sorry to say, not with you. Over to the hotel, you three."

James disengaged himself from Dora, picked up Matthew's hat, which had fallen to the floor, and handed it to his brother. Matthew stepped away from Henri and put his hat on. Shaye noticed he was moving kind of gingerly.

"You all right, Matthew?"

"A little sore in the ribs, Pa," Matthew said. "He hit pretty hard."

"We'll take a look at it back at the hotel," Shaye said, "decide if you need a doctor or not."

120

"I'll be fine, Pa."

James moved around the room, collecting the remainder of the money that was wagered against Matthew, then turned to look at his father with a smile that died quickly.

"Uh, Pa —"

"I'll take that, James," Shaye said. "We can use it to buy some supplies."

"Oh, uh, sure, Pa," James said, handing the money over. "That was what we was figurin', anyway."

"I'm sure you were," Shaye said. "Come on, boys. Let's git."

Matthew turned and waved good-bye to Henri, and then he and James went out the door, followed by Thomas.

"Won't be anymore trouble, Sheriff," Shaye said. "We'll be gone come morning."

Stover nodded, but didn't say a word as Shaye made his way to the door, to follow his sons to the hotel.

24

Matthew bunked with his father that night, so Shaye could check the young man's ribs. They were sore, but he didn't think they were cracked or broken.

"Good thing he didn't hit you twice," Shaye said.

"He hit pretty hard," Matthew said. "I figured I couldn't afford to let him hit me again."

"Smart lad. Better get ready for bed now."

There were two beds in the room. They took turns washing with the pitcher and basin on the dresser, then each climbed into their beds after Shaye doused the light.

"Pa?"

"Yes, Matthew?"

"Sorry about tonight."

"Nothing to be sorry about, Matthew," Shaye said. "Maybe you learned something tonight."

"Maybe I did."

A few moments went by, then Matthew said, "Learned what?" but by then Shaye was snoring.

In the other room, Thomas and James had turned in as well, but neither fell asleep right away.

"Thomas?"

"What?"

"Do you think you're in trouble with Pa?"

"Naw," Thomas said. "Pa didn't seem that upset."

There was a pause, then James asked, "Do you think Pa will ever talk to us about Ma?"

"Yes, James, he will," Thomas said. "He's just not ready yet."

"When do you think he will be ready?"

Thomas pushed himself up on to one elbow and looked at his brother in the other bed. "Probably when we're finished with what we have to do," he answered. "Why, James? Do you want to talk about Ma?"

"All the time."

Thomas laid back down on his back and folded his hands across his belly. "Okay, James," he said, "what do you want to talk about?"

"Well," James said, taking a moment, "do you remember that time when . . ."

■ ■ ■ ■

When they met in the lobby to check out and get some breakfast, Shaye said to Thomas, "You don't look very well rested."

Thomas waited until Matthew and James had gone outside before he answered.

"James kept me up most of the night."

"Snoring?"

"Talkin'."

"About what?"

Thomas hesitated, then said, "Ma."

Shaye put his hand on Thomas's shoulder. "I'm sorry about that, son," he said. "That should be my job. I should be talking to all three of you about her, I guess."

"It's okay, Pa," Thomas said. "I'm the oldest. I can help you with James and Matthew."

"I appreciate that, Thomas. You're a good brother, as well as a good son. But if the boys want to talk about their mother, I guess I should be the one to do it."

"Why can't we both do it, Pa?" Thomas asked. "And why can't Matthew and James talk about Ma between themselves? We can all do it, can't we?"

Shaye clasped his hand on the back of Thomas's neck and said, "Sure, Thomas, we can all do it."

Thomas went outside to join his brothers. Shaye stayed behind a moment. He was proud of Thomas for looking out for his brothers, and he hoped that the boys would talk about their mother among themselves. However, talking to them about their mother's death — that was a father's job. He knew he'd have to find the time to talk to each of the boys alone somewhere along the trail.

Stepping outside, he saw the boys standing together off to one side. Maybe it wasn't fair to make them accompany him on his vendetta, he thought. But they had demanded to come, demanded to be deputized. They hadn't known exactly what they were getting themselves into, but he doubted that any of them would turn back, given the chance.

But perhaps they should be given the chance after all.

"Let's go, boys," he said, joining them. "A good breakfast and we'll be on our way."

"Can't wait to put this town behind us," Matthew said, touching his ribs.

"You did pretty good for yourself, big brother," James said. "Pretty good for all of us. In fact, it's the money we won betting on you that's gonna buy us breakfast — and

I'm havin' a big one!"

They all had big breakfasts and left the café with bulging stomachs.

"Thank you, Matthew," Thomas said. "That was a fine breakfast."

"Pa paid for it," Matthew said.

"Maybe," James said, "but you earned the money."

"And got sore ribs for his trouble," Shaye said. "Maybe I should turn the money over to Matthew."

"All of it?" James asked.

"Well," Shaye said, "maybe what's left after we reoutfit."

They went to the livery for their horses, then rode to the general store to spend some of the money they'd won. They all came out carrying canvas bags which they tied to their saddles, having split all the supplies evenly between them.

As they mounted up to leave, Shaye noticed Sheriff Ray Stover standing out in front of his office, watching them.

"Wait here a second," Shaye told his sons. He turned his horse and directed it over to where the sheriff was standing.

"Sheriff Shaye," Stover said.

"Sheriff Stover."

"Headin' out?"

"That's right."

Ray Stover looked off into the distance. Shaye knew the man had something to tell him, figured he'd let him get to it in his own time.

Finally, Stover looked up at Shaye, who was patiently sitting his horse. "You want to head toward Oklahoma City."

"Is that a fact?"

"Well . . . it's just a feelin' I have, ya know?" Stover said. "Kind of a lawman's feelin'?"

Now it was Shaye's turn to look off into the distance, toward Oklahoma City. "Yes, I know," he said. "I've had those feelings myself."

"I figured you would've."

"Thanks, Sheriff."

"Don't mention it."

Shaye turned his horse, then turned it again so he was facing Stover once more. "You know, if you're lying to me . . ."

"Yes," Stover said, "I know."

Shaye nodded, then turned his horse and rode to join his sons.

25

"Why are we headin' for Oklahoma City?" Terry Petry asked Ethan Langer. "I thought we had to head north to meet the rest."

Langer took a moment before answering Petry. Normally he would have either backhanded the man from his saddle for questioning him or just outright killed him. Aaron, he knew, would have killed Petry without a thought. But then Aaron wasn't having those dreams.

"Ethan?"

"We aren't headin' north, Petry," Langer said. "We're headin' northeast."

"Yeah," Petry said, "but why?"

Langer turned his head to glare at the other man, who had ridden up alongside him to ask him the questions. The other men were laying back, their shoulders hunched against what they thought was coming.

"Since when do I have to explain my

reasons to you, Petry?" he demanded.

"Hey, Ethan," Petry said, "a lot of us are askin' the same question, ya know? I'm the only one figured I could ride up and ask ya without getting' shot."

"Look into my eyes, Terry," Langer said. "Are you still sure that's true?"

Petry did look into Ethan Langer's eyes, and he didn't like what he saw — at all.

"Forget it, Ethan," Petry said. "Just forget it."

"That's right, Terry," Langer said. "You ride back and tell the others to forget it. They can either follow me or go their own way — but if they go, they forfeit their share of the last job. Got it?"

"I got it, Ethan."

"Good, then pass it along."

Petry pulled back and joined the other men, leaving Langer alone with his thoughts — thoughts about his dreams. That woman was still there, every night, screaming in his dreams. He wondered if hearing her scream in real life would have kept him from hearing it in his dreams.

He needed to talk to somebody, but not any of the men he was riding with. He'd considered talking to Aaron, his older brother, except he wasn't sure that Aaron would understand. He didn't even understand. Somebody had to explain it to him, and the only person he knew who could do it lived in Oklahoma City. Once they stopped there, they could still continue north through Indian Territory to meet up with Aaron and his men. Hopefully, by then the woman would be gone from his dreams — and maybe even his dreams would be gone.

Maybe then he'd be able to get some peace in his sleep.

26

The Shayes camped between Lawton and Oklahoma City. There wasn't much else in between the two, but they had outfitted enough in Lawton to be able to make the trip, as long as they rationed their food and drink well enough. Actually, they didn't even need to ration it, just manage it so it would last another hundred miles.

"If they're really going to Oklahoma City, then we're only a couple of days good ride behind them, ain't we, Pa?" James asked.

"That's about right."

"Whether or not we catch up to them," Thomas said, "depends on how long they stay there — that is, if they're really goin' there."

"I think that sheriff was too afraid of Pa to lie to him," Matthew said.

"Is that right, Pa?" James asked. "He was scared of you?"

"Maybe he just wanted to do the right

thing," Shaye said.

"Pa," James said, "tell us some stories about when you was an outlaw."

Shaye looked across the fire at his youngest son.

"Why?" he asked. "Why would you want to hear about a time in my life I'm not proud of?"

"Because you're my pa," James said. "And in the last couple of days I guess I figure we don't know as much about you as we thought we did."

Shaye remained silent.

"And maybe," Thomas said, "maybe we didn't know as much about Ma as we thought we did . . . and now she's dead. Maybe we don't wanna have questions about you, Pa, when you ain't around to answer them."

Now Shaye examined the faces of all three of his sons in the flickering firelight.

"Fair enough," he said at last. "I won't tell stories, but I'll answer your questions."

"Okay," James said, "me first. You ever kill anybody?"

"Before or after I put on a badge?" Shaye asked.

"Not while you've been Sheriff Dan Shaye," Thomas said, "but back when you were Shay Daniels."

Shaye took a deep breath. "Shay Daniels killed some men, yes."

"How many?" Matthew asked.

"To be honest," Shaye said, "I never counted. I never murdered anyone, though. I wasn't that bad. I wasn't Jesse James or Billy the Kid."

"But you were good with a gun?"

Shaye held his right hand out. At the moment it was big, with thick fingers, a powerful hand.

"My hands were different then," he said. "They were like Thomas's hands. That's why Thomas is good with a gun and Matthew isn't."

"And me?" James asked, holding out his hand.

"You have your mother's hands, James."

"Oh, great," he said, drawing his hand back quickly.

"Thomas has her hands too, really, but apparently the speed I had when I was his age. Now my hands are too thick, I often have to double reach for my gun before I get it out of my holster, make sure it's secure in my palm. Back then . . ." His eyes got a faraway look. ". . . I was fast, real fast, and I let it get the better of me."

"How do you mean, Pa?" James asked.

"Like most young men," Shaye said, "I

thought being fast made me special. I thought being able to outdraw other men, and maybe kill them, made me different."

"And it didn't?" Matthew asked.

Again Shaye looked at all his sons before speaking.

"It made me the same as everybody else, boys," he said. "Your mother is the one who made me different, or special. The fact that she chose me made me special. And I learned from her that being able to handle a gun wasn't special at all."

Thomas reached down and touched the smooth handle of his gun. He was fast, and he could hit what he shot at. He thought that made him special. Now he was being told different. If that didn't make him special, then what would? His mother often told him he was special, but he knew she probably said that to Matthew and James as well.

"Did you ride with anyone famous?" James asked Shaye, but Thomas wasn't listening anymore. . . .

Shaye had set watches ever since they left Lawton, mostly for the boys to get into the habit, not because he thought they were in actual danger. There was always a chance the Lawton cowboys might decide they weren't satisfied with the outcome of the arm wrestling incident. There was also the possibility they'd run into Indians — Cheyenne or Arapaho, and later some Cherokee — but there were only four of them and they obviously were not transporting anything of value. Even if and when they turned north and went deep into Indian Territory, Shaye didn't anticipate any problems.

Matthew had first watch, James second, Thomas third. Thomas woke Shaye for the fourth and final watch.

"Get some sleep, Thomas," he said as he settled down by the fire. "We'll get an early start come morning."

"I slept plenty before James woke me," Thomas said. "I'd like to set a while with you, Pa."

"Okay." Shaye knew Thomas had something on his mind. He decided to let his son get to it in his own time. He poured them each a cup of coffee.

"Can I ask you somethin', Pa?"

"You can ask me anything, Thomas."

"Pa, I worked real hard to become good with a gun."

"I know you have, son."

"Why did I do that?"

"You're asking me?"

"Yes, sir."

"You don't know?"

Thomas hesitated, then said, "I thought I did."

"Well, tell me what you thought you knew."

Thomas hesitated again before answering, then said, "I thought it was important."

"Why?"

"Because I wanted to be a lawman, like you."

"Have you? Since when?"

"Since . . . well, I guess since we moved to Texas and you became sheriff."

Shaye recalled that it was only after he started wearing a badge that Thomas began asking for a gun. Mary was worried about that. She didn't want any of her boys to follow in the footsteps of their father — any of the footsteps that he'd left, past, present, or — he assumed — future. Not that she wasn't proud of her husband — she was — but she just didn't want to have to worry about any of her other men . . . when they became men.

She and Shaye had words over when Thomas should be given a handgun, and in the end Shaye's will had prevailed. Thomas began practicing with an unloaded gun when he was thirteen. He got bullets when he turned fifteen. By that time, though, he was a dead shot with a rifle and did much of the hunting for the family.

"So why are you asking the question now, Thomas?"

"Because of what you said earlier," Thomas said, "about being able to handle a gun not making you special."

"You don't need a gun to make you special, Thomas."

The younger Shaye did not respond.

"I see," Shaye said. "You thought it did make you special."

"Yes."

"So now you don't feel special."

Thomas put down his coffee cup and spread his hands. "What is there about me now that makes me special?" he asked.

"First of all," Shaye said, wishing Mary were there to answer the questions, "what makes you think you need to be special? Why can't you just be . . . normal?"

"I . . . don't know," Thomas said. "I just thought . . . it was important."

"And who knows what makes someone special, Thomas?" Shaye said. "You're still young. There is plenty of time for you to . . . become special."

Thomas gazed out into the darkness.

"I wish your mother was here," Shaye

said. "She was so much better at this than I am."

Thomas turned his head and looked at his father. "You're doin' fine, Pa."

"Am I?"

Thomas stood up and patted his father on the shoulder. "Yes, you are. I'll see you in a few hours."

Shaye watched as Thomas walked to his bedroll and rolled himself up in it. His oldest son had just put aside his own questions and doubts to reassure his father about his.

Shaye thought Thomas was pretty special.

27

The Langer gang camped outside of Oklahoma City. In the morning, Ethan told them he was going on alone.

"Alone?" Petry said.

"Yes, alone."

Petry leaned in so he could speak softly. "Ethan, the men were lookin' forward to —"

"I'll talk to the men," Ethan said. He stepped around Petry and approached the others.

"I have somethin' to do in town and I need to do it alone," he said. "It will take me a few hours. If I let all of you ride into a city the size of this one, it'll take me days to round you up again. We can't afford that. We have to meet my brother on time."

"Is stoppin' here gonna make us late?" one man asked.

"No."

"Can't we just go in for —"

139

"No," Ethan said. "Nobody rides in but me. That's it."

He turned and went to saddle his horse.

"This ain't fair," one of the gang members complained to Petry. "There's women in Oklahoma City!"

"What makes you think any of those women would be interested in you, Bates?"

The rest of the men laughed at that.

"That ain't the point!" Bates said.

"Have you got any money?' Petry asked.

"Wha— No, I ain't got any money."

"Anybody else here got any money?" Petry asked.

All of the men shook their heads.

"Do you know why you ain't got any money?"

" 'Cause Ethan's got it all," Bates said. "He's got the money from the bank job."

"Right," Petry said. "So what are any of you gonna do in Oklahoma City without money? You sure ain't gonna get any of them women Bates was talkin' about to look at you without any money. So what's the point of anybody else goin' into town?"

"Ethan's goin' into town!" somebody said.

"He's got a reason."

"What reason?'

"He don't gotta tell us that," Petry said, " 'cause he's the boss. Any of you wanna question him on it personal, be my guest."

The men exchanged looks and shook their heads. Nobody there wanted to take on Ethan Langer.

Horse saddled and ready, Ethan waited a few more moments while Petry finished with the men. Terry Petry had been riding with him for several years now. He'd worked his way up to number two — his *segundo* — when the previous number two man had been killed. Ethan thought that Petry had been a decent second in command up to this point, and there was no one in the gang right now who he would have liked to see move up. If there had been, he might have already killed Petry himself, for questioning him.

As soon as he did find a good replacement, he probably would kill Petry. The man was getting too comfortable in his position — although he had just handled the men pretty well.

Ethan took his horse's reins and walked the animal over to where all the men had gathered.

"Anybody got anything to say?"

The men all shook their heads.

"Well, I got somethin' to say. I'm leavin' the money behind with Petry. If I come back and find it gone, you'll have to deal not only with me, but with my brother. And don't think we won't find you."

Ethan took the two sets of saddlebags filled with money from his saddle and handed them to Petry.

"I know exactly how much money is in there," he said. "If there's a dollar missin', I'll find out who took it and I'll kill him. Do you all understand?"

"Don't worry, Ethan," Petry said, with the saddlebags over his shoulders. "They understand."

Ethan turned and looked directly at Petry. "Do you understand, Terry?"

"Sure I do, Ethan," the man said, almost indignantly. "You know you can count on me."

"I don't even want anybody opening these saddlebags to take a look," Ethan said.

"Nobody's gonna touch 'em, Ethan," Petry said. "I swear."

Ethan switched his gaze back to the men, many of whom were staring at the saddlebags and licking their lips. "I got one other thing to say."

They all looked at him.

"I see any man in town, I'll kill him on the spot, no questions asked. Got it?"

The men nodded that they had it.

Ethan mounted his horse and looked down at them.

"This is gonna be an important test for all of you," Ethan said. "It'll prove your loyalty to both me and my brother." He looked at Petry. "I'll be back before nightfall."

"Don't worry," Petry said. "We'll all be here and so will the money."

"I hope so, Terry," Ethan said. "For everybody's sake."

28

That same morning, two days behind, Dan Shaye woke all three of his sons for breakfast. He had made a full pot of coffee, but it was James's job to actually make breakfast.

Shaye was amazed at how he and his sons were getting along with each other. He knew they all had heavy hearts — no, broken hearts — and he knew they were all filled with anger, but never had that anger spilled over onto each other. Even now, as he watched the three boys picking on each other the way brothers did, he was amazed at their good humor — and at his own.

None of them had been able to mourn yet. That would come later, after the rage was expiated, after the thirst for vengeance was quenched. Once that was done, the emptiness would come, and the tears. Until then he hoped that Mary was looking down at their boys with as much pride as he was.

"Breakfast, Pa!" James called out.

"I'm coming."

Matthew and Thomas saddled the horses while James and Shaye broke camp.

"Can I ask you somethin', Pa?" James asked.

"Always, James," Shaye said, hoping that James's question would be easier to answer than Thomas's last one about being special had been.

"What would Ma think of what we're doin'?"

Shaye sighed. Apparently, his sons were not going to come up with simple questions. "Well, James," he said honestly, "I don't think she'd approve very much."

"Of any of it?"

"No," Shaye said. "She'd approve of me doing my job and trying to get the bank's money back. She would not approve of what I intend to do when I catch up to the Langer gang."

"Kill them?"

"Right. She also would not approve of my taking you boys along with me."

"We got a right."

"She'd probably agree with that part," Shaye said. "Just not with me putting you in danger."

"But you ain't puttin' us in danger," James said. "We're here to watch each other's backs, right? To keep each other safe?"

Shaye finished stomping out the fire and turned to face his youngest son.

"I can't lie to you, James," he said. "We're here to kill the men who killed your ma. At least, that's what I'm here to do."

"Us too."

"No," Shaye said, "it's not the same for you boys as it is for me."

"She was our ma!" James snapped, his face growing red the way his mother's used to when she lost her temper. "We got a right to —"

"Simmer down," Shaye said. "You don't understand. Of course you have a right to come along, but I'm the one who's going to kill them. I'm going to kill Ethan Langer, and probably his brother too. But in the eyes of the law, I might be doing wrong."

"I don't understand."

"What if we catch up to them and they give up?" Shaye asked. "They surrender. What if they'd rather go to jail than resist and possibly die?"

James looked confused. He didn't have any answers. "Would you still kill them, Pa?"

"Yes, James, I would, and I will."

"But . . . wouldn't that be murder?"

"In the eyes of the law, yes it would be," Shaye said. "But James, murder is what I've been planning ever since we left Epitaph."

29

While Dan Shaye and his sons continued on toward Oklahoma City, Ethan Langer rode into that city with a definite goal in mind. He had to find somebody, get his question answered, and get back to camp before nightfall. He thought he had his men sufficiently cowed to keep them from looking in the saddlebags he'd left in Terry Petry's hands, but it was hard to be sure.

Oklahoma City was larger than the towns Langer was used to spending time in. His older brother, Aaron, liked big cities, like Denver and Chicago. Ethan preferred smaller, more western towns to spend his time in.

He knew the place he was looking for, he just didn't know where it was. He stopped a man and a woman on the street to ask them, because they looked like the type of people who would know. After giving him a startled look — he knew he looked trail weary —

they were happy to direct him.

"The Church of the Holy Redeemer is on the other side of the square, sir," the woman said. The man took over then and gave him directions. Langer thanked them politely so he wouldn't stand out in their minds, in case anyone asked, mounted his horse and followed the directions to the church.

Terry Petry sat at the first fire with the saddlebags at his feet. While he was pleased that Ethan had entrusted the money to him, he knew that the other men were now sizing him up, trying to decide if they should make a move for the money. All six of them were seated around the second fire, watching him. Of course, they also had to decide if they wanted to risk the wrath of both Ethan and Aaron Langer by going for the money.

If they did go for it, though, Petry knew he was the one who was going to end up dead, but he'd take some of those sonsof-bitches with him. He wasn't going alone.

Eventually, one man, Ted Fitzgerald, separated himself from the others and came walking over. He'd been riding with Ethan's gang the least of anyone, and this had only been his second job.

"Hey, Petry, some of us have been talkin'," Fitzgerald said as he approached.

"Looks to me like all of you have been talkin'," Petry said, "and I think I know what about."

"What's the harm in jest takin' a little look-see, ya know?" Fitzgerald asked, standing by the fire now.

"Forget it, Fitz," Petry said, "and tell the rest to forget it too. Ethan left this in my care, and if anyone looks inside, it's my head."

"We could take it from you, ya know."

"You could try," Petry said, "but I'd kill some of ya, and the rest of ya would have to deal with Ethan and Aaron trackin' ya down. You want that, Fitz?"

Fitzgerald looked more frustrated than angry. "It ain't fair," he said. "We don't even know how much we got from that bank."

"We don't never know until Ethan and Aaron get together," Petry said. "They like to see which one got the most money, first. Just go on back to the others, Fitz, and tell 'em we're gonna wait until we meet up with Aaron, like always."

"Can't even take a look, huh?"

"Not even a look."

Fitzgerald kicked at the ground, then turned and walked back to the others. He hunkered down by the fire and they all started talking again. Petry was pretty sure there were only one or two who were pushing the others to make a move. The rest of them were too smart to risk going against the Langers.

Petry poured himself a cup of coffee and kept it in his left hand so his right hand — his gun hand — was free.

He hoped Ethan would get back soon.

Ethan Langer reined his horse in outside the Church of the Holy Redeemer, dismounted and went inside. It was a big stone church, with high ceilings, and it was so empty that he could hear his own footsteps echoing throughout.

He stopped just inside, unsure of what to do. He removed his hat, held it in both hands. It was midday, middle of the week, so he guessed people didn't come to church much at this time of the day. That would probably work in his favor.

He finally decided nothing would happen if he didn't at least move away from the door. He started down the center aisle, knowing there was something he should be doing but unsure what. It had been a long time since he'd been in a church.

When he reached the front, he looked up at the altar and the image of Christ on the cross behind it. Off to one side he heard some footsteps, and turned to see a man coming though a door from somewhere in the back. The man was in his late forties, dressed all in black, with a white collar. He stopped short when he saw Ethan standing there.

"You have the gall to come here?" he demanded.

"What's the matter?" Ethan asked. "A man ain't allowed to visit his own brother?"

30

The two men faced each other in the empty church.

"You're no brother of mine," Father Vincent said. Once, he'd been Vincent Langer, older brother of Ethan and younger brother of Aaron. "You and Aaron gave up the right to call me brother when you turned to a life of crime."

"Okay," Ethan said, "then I didn't come here as your brother."

"What then?"

"I came because I need the help . . . of a priest."

Vincent frowned. "You're joking with me."

"Why would I come here to make a joke, Vincent?"

"Father Vincent!"

"Okay, Father Vincent."

Vincent studied Ethan for several seconds before coming closer. He stopped about five feet away, still looking his brother up and down.

"Is it true, then?" he asked finally. "You've come to me for spiritual guidance?"

"I don't know if that's what it's called," Ethan said, "but I need some kind of help."

"Do you want to confess?"

"No, Vin— Father Vincent," Ethan said. "I just want to talk."

"All right, then," Father Vincent said, "all right. We'll sit down here and talk, Ethan. If it's help you need, I cannot in all good conscience turn you away, can I?"

"I hope not," Ethan said, "because if you can't help me, I don't know where I'll go."

"Pa?"

Here it comes, Shaye thought. The only one who hadn't asked any questions yet — serious questions — was Matthew, and he had just ridden up alongside him. Thomas and James were riding behind them.

"Yes, Matthew?"

"Can I ask you somethin'?"

"Sure, Matthew," Shaye said. "Go ahead and ask."

"James told me and Thomas that you said what you're gonna do to the men who killed Ma is murder."

"That's right, Matthew," Shaye said. "The law might consider it murder, depending on how things go."

"But how could that be?" he asked, clearly puzzled. "Ain't we got a right to avenge our ma?"

"We got rights, Matthew," Shaye said. "Maybe not in the eyes of the law, but in our own eyes."

"But if the law considers it murder, are you gonna do it anyway?"

"Yes, I am."

"But you're a lawman, Pa," Matthew said. "How can you break the law?"

"It's not something I want to do, son," Shaye said. "I've been upholding the law for the past twelve years. Don't forget, I broke the law for some time before that."

"But you're wearin' a badge now."

"Yes, I am."

"And you'd still do it?"

"Yes, I would."

"But . . . why?"

"Because I answer to a higher law, Matthew," Shaye said.

"Whose law is that, Pa? God's?"

"No, Matthew," Shaye said, "not God's law. My own."

Matthew thought about that for a few moments, then shook his head and said, "I don't think I understand, Pa."

"Let me try to explain it to you, then. . . ."

■ ■ ■ ■

"My God," Father Vincent said after Ethan told him what had been bothering him, "do you mean to say you killed a woman while robbing a bank?"

"No," Ethan said, "she got killed while we were escapin', not while we were robbin' the bank."

"I can't believe what I am hearing."

"And I didn't kill her," Ethan went on, "she ran out in front of my horse."

"My God, man," Father Vincent said, "you rode her down and killed her."

"Others rode over her too," Ethan said. "Why am I the only one dreamin' about her?"

"It's the guilt, man," Father Vincent said, "the guilt over having killed a woman."

"Why is she screamin' in my dream?" Ethan asked. "She didn't scream in the street."

"It's the guilt that makes you hear her scream —"

"Stop sayin' that!" Ethan shouted, jumping to his feet. "I don't feel guilty! The damn woman ran out in front of us. Any one of us coulda rode her down first."

"Why did you come here, then, Ethan?"

his brother asked. "Why, if you feel no guilt, did you come to me?"

" 'Cause there ain't no one else I can go to," Ethan said.

"There's Aaron."

"He'd laugh at me."

"Friends?"

"They'd laugh too."

"Then they're not really friends."

"That don't matter," Ethan said. "Vincent — Father Vincent — tell me what to do to stop the screams."

"I'm afraid there isn't much I can tell you, Ethan," Vincent said. "I believe you will have the dreams until you admit your guilt and turn yourself in."

"What? I ain't gonna turn myself in. Jesus, why would I do a thing like that?"

"To rid yourself of the dreams."

Ethan stared at Vincent for a few moments, obviously trying to comprehend what his brother was telling him.

"So that's the only way?"

"The only way I can see."

"Well," Ethan said after a moment, "I guess I'll just have to learn to live with it, then."

Father Vincent stood up and put his hand on his brother's arm. "There's no way you can live with something like that, Ethan," he warned. "It will continue to eat away at you for the rest of your life."

"I'll live with it, Vincent," Ethan said, pulling his arm away, " 'cause I ain't gonna do none of that other stuff you just told me to do. No way in hell!"

Ethan put his hat back on, turned and started walking back up the aisle.

"Ethan," Vincent said, "I beg you, admit the guilt. Take responsibility for what you did. It's the only way to save your soul."

"It ain't my soul I was worried about, Vincent," Ethan shouted from the back of the church. "It was my mind."

31

"I loved your mother more than anything, Matthew," Shaye said, trying to explain himself to his middle son. "I loved her more than any law created by God or man, and I'll break any or all of those laws avenging her death. It's as simple as that."

"But won't you go to jail?"

"Maybe."

"And that don't matter to you?"

"No."

"What about us?"

"What about you?"

"Don't you love us?"

"Of course I do."

"Well," Matthew said, "if you go to jail, what are we gonna do without a ma and a pa?"

"Matthew," Shaye said, "you and your brothers are grown men. You don't need a mother and father around to tell you what to do anymore."

"Maybe Thomas don't," Matthew said, "or James, but me, I ain't smart like them, Pa. What am I gonna do if you go to jail?"

Shaye hesitated, then said, "Thomas will look after you, Matthew. He's the oldest and he'll look after the both of you."

"Will you tell him that?" Matthew asked.

"I'll tell him."

Matthew hesitated a moment, then said, "Okay." He dropped back to ride with his brothers again.

There was another eventuality that Shaye had not discussed with Matthew. In fact, there were more than one.

First, there was the possibility that he might get killed while trying to avenge Mary's death. Oh, he'd take those evil sons-ofbitches with him if he could, but instead of going to jail, he might just outright get himself killed.

And on the other hand, since he had his three sons with him, one, two, or all of them might get killed as well.

Was he willing to sacrifice his sons — any or all of them — to avenge his wife's death?

Were his sons willing to die — or watch their father die — to avenge their mother?

Was he willing to ask himself these questions, and answer them, if it meant giving up his hunt, his vendetta?

160

At the moment he had to admit that he wasn't. Leave it to Matthew — the simplest, most innocent of the brothers — to come up with the hardest questions of all.

Questions Dan Shaye was certainly not ready to answer.

32

It was getting dark, and apparently the other men had decided it was not worth risking their lives to take the saddlebags from Terry Petry. Petry was still sitting at the fire with the bags between his legs, but at the moment no one was looking at him.

He'd been staring down at the saddlebags, observing the way they were buckled. It wouldn't be too hard to unbuckle them — maybe just on one side — and take a peek at the money. He had to admit he really wanted a looksee. Now that nobody was watching him he could just reach down and undo one buckle.

He decided to try it. He kept a cup of coffee in one hand and slid the other hand down along his leg. When he reached one of the saddlebags, he slowly undid one buckle. He figured he could lift one end of the flap and just take a quick look inside with no one being the wiser.

When he got the buckle undone he looked over at the other men to be sure they were still not looking his way. Satisfied that he had gone undetected this far, he looked down, lifted one side of the flap, and took a look inside.

He was not at all prepared for what he saw.

When Ethan Langer rode back into camp, he was not in a good mood. He had not gotten what he wanted from his brother the priest, and so had wasted time bringing himself and his men to Oklahoma City. He should have shot up that damn church, he thought, that's what he should have done. Maybe that would have made him feel better.

But that would not have done anything for his dreams. Could Vincent have been right? Would this woman never stop haunting his dreams? Was he never to have a good night's sleep again?

When he rode into camp, all the men looked up at him, but he ignored them and rode by. He dismounted and began to unsaddle his horse when Terry Petry came over.

"Ethan we gotta talk."

"About what?"

"About the money."

"What about it, Terry?"

"Well . . ."

Ethan turned away from his horse and looked at Terry Petry. "You looked, didn't you?" he asked.

"I —"

"You looked in the saddlebags."

"I — uh, just one."

"And what did you see?"

"Nothin'!" Petry said. "I mean, there ain't no money in them, just some rocks and stuff."

"To make them heavy," Ethan said, "and to make them look nice and full."

"But Ethan . . . where's the money?"

Ethan went back to caring for his horse. "I hid it."

"Where?"

"If I told you that," Ethan said, "then it wouldn't be hid anymore, would it?"

"But . . . why?"

"To test you," Ethan said, "and to test the other men. Did any of them look in it?"

"No," Petry said, "they wanted to, but I didn't let them."

"That was good."

"I know —"

"But you looked in the saddlebags," Ethan said, finished with his horse and turning to look at Petry.

"Well, I — uh, yeah, I just, uh, lifted one flap of one saddlebag and sort of . . . peeked."

"That was bad, Terry."

"Why?"

" 'Cause that means that while I can trust the rest of the men," Ethan said, "I can't trust you, and you're my second in command. You're the one I'm supposed to be able to trust."

"Well, I, uh, just wanted to make sure the, uh, money was all there —" Petry started.

"Why, Terry?" Ethan asked, cutting him off. "Why would you want to do that?"

"I, uh —"

"Don't you trust me?"

"Well, sure —"

"So you trust me," Ethan said, "and I trust the rest of the men. Seems the only one around here who ain't trustworthy is you."

Plus he was going to keep on having these dreams about the dead woman until who knew when? Since he hadn't shot up the church — and he couldn't very well shoot his own brother, whether he was a priest or not — he did the next best thing in order to blow off the steam that was building inside of him.

He drew his gun and shot Terry Petry
dead.

33

When Shaye and his sons camped that night, the three boys were quiet. Shaye was quiet as well. He assumed they were all spending some time with their own thoughts.

In the past few days or so he'd done a piss-poor job of answering his sons' questions. Now, their mother, she knew how to answer them when they had questions. She was able to satisfy them with her answers, set aside whatever fears they had, and make them feel better.

He felt sorely lacking in that area.

The boys were probably now convinced that he was some kind of amoral ex-outlaw who was going to turn to murder to achieve his goal. One man's murder, though, was another man's justice. Was that something he'd be able to make the three boys understand when the time came?

Perhaps it was time to give them an opportunity to change their minds. Now that they knew what he was planning, maybe they wouldn't be so eager to follow him anymore.

He decided the only way to find out was to ask them. They were, after all — as he had told Matthew — grown men, with their own minds to make up.

He waited until they were seated around the campfire, finished eating and drinking coffee.

"I want to talk to you boys about something," he said.

"What's that, Pa?"

"Since we left Epitaph, you boys have found out some things you didn't know before."

"What kind of things, Pa?" Matthew asked.

"Things about me," Shaye said. "About the man I used to be, and about what I plan to do when we finally catch up to the Langer gang."

"Pa," Thomas said, "we knew when we left town what we were going to do when we found them."

"But you didn't know that the law might look at it as murder."

"Well . . . no . . ." Thomas said.

"Now that you know," Shaye said, "I think

168

you three should be offered the opportunity to make up your own minds."

"About what, Pa?" James asked. "Specifically?"

"About whether or not to continue with me," Shaye said. "I'm offering you the opportunity to turn back if you want to."

"Turn back?" James asked.

"And go where?" Thomas asked. "To Epitaph?"

"Well —"

"There's nothin' for us in Epitaph, Pa," Thomas said. "Ma's dead. The only family we have is you, and we're stayin' with you — at least, I'm stayin' with you. You're givin' us the chance to make up our own minds, so I've made my decision."

Shaye looked at his middle son. "Matthew?"

"I'm stayin' with you, Pa."

"James?"

"Me too," the younger brother said. "No question."

"Boys . . . there's a possibility that the law might come after you too."

"We'll be ready for them, Pa," Thomas said.

"We got a right to avenge our mother," James said, "and your wife. Do any of us doubt that?"

Matthew and Thomas both shook their heads no. There was no doubt whatsoever.

"We'll deal with that when the time comes, Pa," Thomas said. "We got somethin' to do, and we're gonna do it."

"With you," Matthew said. "Where you go, we go, and what you do, we're gonna do."

Well, there was some doubt about that in Shaye's mind, but what he said was, "Thank you, boys."

"You don't gotta thank us, Pa," Matthew said. "She was our ma."

Thomas and James nodded their agreement.

"You're good —" Shaye stopped himself. "I was just going to say that you're good boys, but that's wrong. The three of you are all good men now."

"You and Ma did a good job raisin' us, Pa," Thomas said.

"Your mother did all the work."

"Not true, Pa," Thomas said. "Maybe she was home all the time and you weren't, but we learned a lot from you, just from watchin' you . . . just from the kind of man you are."

"It doesn't matter what kind of man you were once, Pa," James said. "It only matters what kind of man you been to us, what kind of father. I don't think we could have had a better one."

Thomas and Matthew nodded their agreement.

Shaye stared at all three of his sons with pride. If he had even the smallest amount to do with them becoming the men they were, he was also proud of himself.

"We're all good men," Matthew said proudly.

Thomas picked up the coffeepot and poured all their cups full so they could toast that fact. Privately, Dan Shaye wondered who else would be convinced of that once they had successfully done what they had set out to do.

34

When morning came, the other men in the Langer gang were still stunned by what had happened the night before. They only had to look over at the mound of dirt and stones they had piled atop Terry Petry's body to remind themselves.

None of the men had spoken with Ethan Langer since he pulled the trigger on Petry. Ethan had told them to bury Petry, and asked if any of them had any questions for him about why he killed him.

"If you do," he'd said, "ask them now, but remember what I told you all when I left camp. If anyone looked in those saddlebags, I was gonna kill 'em. Somebody looked inside, and I think it was Petry. Anyone else want to admit to it? Tell me I killed the wrong man?"

They had all shaken their heads.

"Fine," he'd said, "then bury him, and somebody make somethin' to eat. I'm hungry."

Now, in the morning light, some of them had some questions, but they were wary of asking Ethan Langer anything. The same person who made dinner the night before made breakfast, and they all sat and ate in silence.

It was Ethan who broke that silence.

"Listen up," he said. "In a few minutes we're gonna head north to meet up with my brother Aaron. Petry was my *segundo,* and now he's dead. Ain't none of you fit to take his place, but a leader needs a *segundo.* I'll decide later who it'll be, maybe when we join up with my brother. Until then, you'll all do what I say when I say it. Is that clear?"

They all nodded. Ethan had recovered the money from where he'd hidden it and had put it back in the saddlebags. Now he held up the bags.

"The money is in these saddlebags, and you'll all get your share when we get where we're going. If any of you wants to leave us now, you can, but you won't get your share. Anybody got anything to say?"

They all shook their heads. There were six of them, and he was just one man. If he had been one of them, he would have made a move already. For all of them to be afraid of one man was ridiculous, but they were.

"Anybody want to leave?"

Nobody did.

"Good," he said. "Then we understand each other. Break camp and get saddled up. We're leaving."

As they broke camp, Red Hackett said to the others under his breath, "He's just one man. We could take the money from him if we want to."

"Hackett is right," Ted Fitzgerald said. "There's plenty of money there for all of us, and with Petry and Langer dead, we get even bigger splits."

"We also get Aaron Langer after us," another man said, "and believe me, if you think Ethan is bad, Aaron is worse."

The other men nodded their agreement.

"So we just do what we're told?" Fitzgerald asked.

Ben Branch had been riding with the Langers for a long time. "Hey," he said, "I joined up because I wanted to follow somebody I trusted. I trusted both Ethan and Aaron Langer to line my pockets with money, and that's what they been doin.' I don't give a good goddamn when I get the money or who the *segundo* of this group is."

"Don't you want to be a leader instead of

a follower?" Hackett asked.

"Hell, no!" Branch said. "You and Fitz want to be leaders? You take Ethan on. It'll be two against one."

"Six against one would work better," Fitzgerald hissed.

Branch looked right at both Red Hackett and Ted Fitzgerald and said, "That ain't gonna happen."

They broke camp and rode out with Ethan Langer in the lead. The woman had come to him again last night, but he had come awake slowly and not with a start, like he usually did. Maybe he could just accept her as part of his life now. Maybe if he stopped fighting her, she'd go away.

He knew the men had to have had a discussion while saddling their horses about whether to take the money from him, yet while riding in front of them he had no fear of a bullet in the back. Several of them had been with him a long time — Branch and a few of the others. Red Hackett had been with him only a year, and Epitaph had been Ted Fitzgerald's second job. If a challenge was going to come, it would come from one or both of them — but neither struck him as the type who would act without a lot of backup.

Once they met up with Aaron and his group, he needed to reevaluate who he kept in his gang. Hackett and Fitzgerald were going to go. He'd keep the other four, and while he told them that none of them was fit to be *segundo,* maybe he'd just give the job to whoever had been with him the longest — like Ben Branch.

As they headed north Ethan realized this was the first morning since the bank job that he felt calm. Maybe going to see his brother Vincent had been the right thing to do after all.

35

As the Shayes rode into Oklahoma City, the three younger men looked around them, almost in awe. Most of their lives had been spent in small towns like Epitaph, and they were surprised by the sheer size of this place.

"How are we gonna find out if they were here?" James asked.

"Well," Shaye said, "luckily, I know a little something about the Langer brothers."

"Like what?" Thomas asked.

Shaye looked at him and said, "Like there's three of them."

They registered at a hotel, taking two rooms with two beds each, but Shaye kept them from boarding their horses.

"Why are we keepin' them?" Thomas asked.

"We need to go and see someone," Shaye said, "and originally I was going to go alone, but I think you b— the three of you deserve to know what I know." He didn't feel justified in calling them "boys" anymore, even though they would always be his boys.

"Which is?" Thomas asked.

"Come along and I'll show you."

They reined their horses in outside the Church of the Holy Redeemer.

"We're goin' to church?" Matthew asked as they dismounted.

"Only to see someone, Matthew," Shaye said.

They followed their father into church. By coincidence, it was roughly the same time of day that Ethan Langer had entered a day earlier. The church was empty, and the scuffling footsteps of the four men echoed throughout the place.

They felt funny being inside the church. With the death of his wife, Shaye's belief that there was a benevolent God had been sorely tested and had come up wanting. If there was a God, he now believed Him to be cruel.

Thomas felt much the same way his father did, that a God who was good as priests had been telling him all his life would not have taken his mother.

James and Matthew both dipped their fingers in holy water and made the sign of the cross while genuflecting, purely from habit. They had not quite come to terms with the responsibility God might have had for their mother's death.

"Where do we go?" James asked in a whisper.

"Let's go right down the center and see what happens," Shaye said in his normal tone.

By the time they reached the altar, the sacristy door opened and a man came out. He wore black and a cleric's collar.

"Can I help you?" he asked.

The four men turned to face him. The priest studied the faces of the three younger men before moving on to Shaye's. When he saw him, he stopped short and squinted.

"My God!" he breathed. "Shay Daniels?"

"It's Dan Shaye now, Vincent," Shaye said.

"And it's Father Vincent," the priest said. He seemed to suddenly become aware of the badges all four men were wearing. "Oh, no. Are you here for . . . ?"

"We're looking for Ethan, Vin— Father Vincent," Shaye said. "Has he been here?"

Thomas, James, and Matthew watched the two men with interest. Obviously, they knew each other from another time, and just as obviously there was still more to be discovered about their father.

"Danny —"

"Dan," Shaye said, "or Sheriff."

"Sheriff of . . . what town?"

"Epitaph, Texas. Ethan and his men hit the bank in my town."

Father Vincent hesitated, then said, "The woman . . ."

"Was my wife."

The priest closed his eyes and shook his head. "I'm so sorry. . . ."

"What about Ethan, Father?"

"Yes, yes," Father Vincent said, "he was here yesterday."

"Yesterday!" Matthew said, excited.

"We're only a day behind, Pa," James said.

"What did he say?" Shaye asked Father Vincent.

"He came to ask me . . . he said he was being haunted by . . . by a woman. . . ."

"Mary."

"He said she came to him in his dreams."

"Good," Shaye said. "I hope she never stops."

"I told him the only way to stop the dreams was to confess his guilt and surrender himself."

"He's not going to do that."

"No," the priest agreed, "he is not."

"Did he say where he was going when he left here?" Shaye asked.

"No, but I assume he's going to meet with Aaron," Father Vincent said. "I mean, isn't

180

that their pattern?"

"Yes."

"So Aaron hit a bank in . . . ?"

"South Dakota."

"Did he kill anyone?"

"I don't know," Shaye said. "This time."

Father Vincent's legs seemed to suddenly give out and he sat down heavily in a front pew.

Shaye moved closer. "I'm going to get him, Vincent," he said. "I'm going to track him down and get him."

The man looked up. "And what will you do when you find him, Daniel?" he asked. "Arrest him?"

"Kill him."

"That is not your job."

"I've made it my life's goal."

"To kill?"

"Yes."

Father Vincent looked up at the crucifix behind the altar. "God —" he started, but got no further.

"Don't talk to me about God, Vincent," Shaye said savagely. "God sent your brother to my town to kill my wife. If there is a God, then He's sending me to kill your brother."

"No," Father Vincent said. "He doesn't do that."

"What does He do, Father?"

They both looked at Thomas, who had spoken.

"What does God do?" Thomas asked again. "If he didn't send your brother to kill my mother, why did it happen?"

"The ways of the Lord are mysterious, my son —"

"Don't call me that!" Thomas said. He pointed to Shaye. "That man is my father, and I have more faith in him than in any God who would let my mother be killed . . . and be killed in that way —"

Thomas stopped, then abruptly turned, walked up the aisle and out of the church.

"Pa —" James said.

"Go with your brother," Shaye said, "both of you. I'll be out in a minute."

James and Matthew both nodded, followed in their brother's wake and left the church.

"They're angry," Father Vincent said.

"The four of us are angry," Shaye said, "and frustrated. We haven't had any time to grieve. And we won't grieve until your brother is dead, Vincent."

"And what about Aaron?" the priest asked.

"Him too, if he's there when we catch up to them."

"How can you do this to your sons, Daniel?" the priest asked. "You'll make murder-

182

ers of them."

"I'm going to pull the trigger on Ethan, Vincent," Shaye said, "not my sons. They are duly sworn-in deputies, acting as a posse to pursue a gang of bank robbers."

"Out of your jurisdiction."

"That may be," Shaye said, "but when they pull the trigger, it will be in self-defense."

"And when you pull the trigger on Ethan?" Father Vincent asked. "What will that be?"

"That will be vengeance, pure and simple."

"Some would call it murder."

"I'm prepared for that."

"I feel sorry for you, Daniel," Vincent said. "You've lost your way —"

"Feel sorry for your brother, Vincent," Shaye said. "When I catch up to him, he's going to need your sympathy. Can you tell me where he went?"

"No," Father Vincent said. "Because I don't know."

"Would you tell me if you did know?"

"I would not."

"To protect your brother?"

Father Vincent shook his head. "To protect you and your sons. To keep you from doing something that may damn you —"

"I'm already damned, Father," Shaye said.

He turned and stalked up the middle aisle to the back door. He was stopped by the priest's voice, echoing from the front of the church.

" 'Vengeance is mine sayeth the Lord,' Daniel!"

Shaye turned and shouted back, "He's going to have to fight me for it!"

36

Outside, in front of the church, Shaye found his sons standing apart, Thomas off to one side with his head bowed, James and Matthew together on another side, looking away from their brother. Like most young men — and possibly like most men — they had not learned how to deal with intense emotions yet. The emotions that Thomas was feeling at the moment embarrassed his brothers. Shaye walked over to his oldest son and put his hand on his shoulder.

"I'm sorry, Pa."

"For what?" Shaye asked. "Speaking your mind? Don't ever be sorry about that, Thomas."

"Ma was a churchgoin' woman," Thomas said. "She'd'a tanned me good for talkin' to a priest that way."

"There's absolutely nothing wrong with having your faith tested, Thomas."

Thomas looked at his father. "Is your faith

being tested, Pa?"

"Sorely tested, Thomas," Shaye said truthfully. "In fact, my faith is shaken."

"What do we do about it?"

"We can't dwell on it now, son," Shaye said. "It would keep us from doing what has to be done."

"So what do we do?"

"We set the question aside for another time," Shaye said. "Come on, let's go talk to your brothers."

James and Matthew had been having a conversation of their own about faith.

" 'Course there's a God, James," Matthew said. "How could we be here if there wasn't?"

"I don't know, Matthew," James said. "I just know that Ma didn't deserve what happened to her. How could God do that?"

"God didn't do it," Matthew said, "the Langer gang did, and we're gonna kill them for it. We can't blame God, 'cause then we'd have to kill God for it, and we can't kill God." Matthew's logic made perfect sense to him.

"We could stop believin' in Him," James said.

"James," Matthew said, "if Ma ever heard you say that —"

Shaye and Thomas joined them then, and both James and Matthew looked embarrassed about their own conversation.

"You two okay?" Shaye asked.

"We're fine, Pa," James said. "Thomas?"

"I'm fine."

"You've probably already figured this out," Shaye said, "but I knew Vincent Shaye — Father Vincent — years ago, which means I also knew Ethan and Aaron."

"During your outlaw days?" Matthew asked.

"Yes, Matthew," Shaye said. "We crossed paths during my outlaw days."

"So you knew why Langer was headin' for Oklahoma City," Thomas said.

"Not really, but I figured while he was here he might stop to see his brother."

"What did the father mean about Langer seein' Ma in his dreams, Pa?" Matthew asked.

"Your mother is haunting Ethan Langer, Matthew," Shaye said. "He's dreaming about her at night."

"Good for Ma!" James said.

"Father Vincent seems to think this is the way Ethan is dealing with his guilt."

"The important thing," Thomas said, "is that we're only a day behind the gang."

"Yes, Thomas," Shaye said, "that is important, but we also need rest, and so do the horses, so we'll be staying overnight."

"But we'll lose some of the ground we've made up," James said.

"We're going to catch up to them, James," Shaye said. "That's a foregone conclusion. They can't get away from us. A half a day this way or that isn't going to make much difference."

"So what do we do now?" Matthew asked.

"We go back to our hotel, we board the horses, and we get something to eat," Shaye said.

"Good," Matthew said, "because I'm starvin'."

"You're always starvin'," James said as they mounted their horses. "If you ever weren't starvin', I'd think you weren't my brother anymore."

Inside the church, Father Vincent rose from the pew he was sitting in, went to the altar and knelt before it. He had to pray, but he wasn't really sure who or what to pray for. His brothers were evil men. Should he pray for their souls? Daniel Shaye and his sons were after vengeance, but they weren't bad men. Pray for them?

He made the sign of the cross and pressed his hands together. Maybe he'd just play it safe and pray for all of them — and while he was at it, toss in a prayer for himself as well.

37

They all had steak dinners that night, and there wasn't much conversation during the meal. Shaye had the feeling they were all having thoughts about faith and religion. He was starting to wonder if accompanying him on his vendetta was going to adversely effect them as men. Or should he simply stop thinking about this as something he had to do and start thinking of it as something *they* all had to do — *their* vendetta? After all, they had as much right to it as he did.

During dessert, however, it was Matthew who finally brought the question of religion up.

"Pa?

"Yes, Matthew?"

"Do you not believe in God anymore?"

Thomas stole a quick look at his father and James looked away. He was hoping Matthew wouldn't tell their father what he had said about that subject earlier in the day.

"Matthew," Shaye said, "I don't think we can give God much thought until we've accomplished what we've set out to do."

"How can we do that?" Matthew asked.

"It won't be easy, but we have to try," Shaye said. "If any one of us can't put aside the question of God while we're doing this, he's going to have to turn back."

Matthew looked confused.

"Can you do that, Matthew?"

"I don't know, Pa," Matthew said, "but I know I don't wanna turn back."

"Just give it some thought tonight, then," Shaye said. "God would not approve of what we're doing, and your mother certainly would not approve. But we can't dwell on that. We have to be committed to this, or even when we catch up to them and there's the slightest doubt about what we're doing, we could end up dead."

"I'm committed, Pa," Thomas said. "We have to do this, no matter what anyone thinks."

"Me too," James said.

Matthew looked panic stricken and confused. He wasn't sure he agreed with the rest of his family, he wasn't sure he even knew what the word "committed" meant, but he knew that he could not turn back on his own.

"Matthew," Shaye said, "no one wants to force you into anything. You could stay here and wait for us to come back —"

"I ain't never been on my own, Pa," Matthew said. "I wouldn't know what to do. I gotta come along."

"Well then, you and I will have to keep talking about it along the way, Matthew," Shaye said. "You've got to be absolutely convinced you're doing the right thing, or I don't want you to do it."

"The right thing is for me to come with you."

"Son," Shaye said, "that's just not a good enough reason to kill someone, and that's what we're aiming to do."

Thomas reached over and put his hand on his brother's shoulder. "We'll all talk about it, Matthew."

"We're not gonna leave you behind," James assured him.

"Damn right you're not," Matthew said. "You guys would get in too much trouble without me."

"And we know it!" James agreed.

"Like that time . . ." Matthew went on, and Shaye was happy to see the conversation take a new course.

He had to make sure that by the time they caught up to the gang, they were all ready to do what had to be done. The slightest hesitation on any of their parts could end up being a disaster for all of them.

Matthew's face was still a little pale even as he started to banter with his brothers.

"How about some pie?" Shaye asked.

Matthew smiled and said, "Now you're talkin'!"

38

With Petry dead, Ethan Langer actually started to miss having someone to talk to, even if it was just to tell him to shut up. For that reason he decided to start talking to Ben Branch.

As they crossed into Kansas he said, "Ben, I'm actually thinkin' of making you my *segundo.*"

Branch was surprised. "But you said none of us was good enough."

"Well, maybe I was wrong," Ethan said. "Maybe you're good enough. What do you think?"

"I been real happy just following you along these past few years, Ethan," Branch said. "I ain't really got no hankerin' to give any orders, myself."

"You wouldn't have to give no orders, Ben," Ethan said. "That's still my job."

Branch remembered what happened to the last *segundo* when Ethan left him in charge for just a little while. Terry Petry earned himself a real shallow grave. Branch was sure that a bunch of critters had already taken care of Petry's remains.

"Whataya say, Ben?" Ethan asked. "Want the job or not?"

"Well, Ethan —"

"There's an extra share in it for you," Ethan said. "Petry's share."

Well, if there was extra money in it for him, that was a whole different story.

"Sure, Ethan," Branch said, "I'd be happy to be your *segundo.*"

"Good," Ethan said. "Then you ride back and tell the rest of the men about it, and then come back up here."

"Right, boss."

"He made you *segundo*?" Hackett asked.

"That's right."

"Did you ask for the job?" Ted Fitzgerald asked suspiciously.

"Hell, no," Branch said. "I saw what happened to Petry."

"So why'd you say yes?"

"How could I say no?" Branch asked. He didn't want to tell them about the extra share. "I didn't want to get blown out of my saddle."

195

"So what's he want you to do?" Hackett asked.

"Just ride with him," Branch said, "and that's what I'm gonna do."

Well," Hackett said, "if he asks you for any advice, why don't you suggest we stop off in Dodge City? It ain't far from here."

"He ain't gonna ask," Branch said, "but I'll keep it in mind."

When he rode back up to ride alongside his boss, Ethan asked, "How did they take it?"

"They took it fine."

"Anybody mention Dodge City?"

Branch looked surprised.

Ethan laughed. "We ain't far from there. I figured somebody would suggest it.'

"Somebody did."

"Dodge is a dead town," Ethan said. "Besides, we ain't stoppin' anymore until we get where we're goin'."

"Where are we goin', Ethan?" Branch asked, and then hurriedly added, "Uh, I mean, if I can ask."

"Aaron and I agreed on where we'd meet, and when," Ethan said. "We'll be a little late, but he'll wait for us to get there."

"I know he will," Branch said. "Think we got more from our bank than he got from his?"

"That'll burn his ass if we do," Ethan said. "Guess we'll find out when we get there."

"Uh, get where, Ethan?"

"Salina, *segundo*," Ethan said. "We're goin' to Salina."

39

They stopped in Blackwell, just before the Kansas border. Prior to that they had a small run-in with a Cherokee hunting party. There were six braves, and they were looking for food. Shaye calmed his sons, who had only seen Indians before one at a time, and the tame variety at that. Shaye satisfied the braves with some beef jerky, and they all went their separate ways. Thomas, Matthew, and James talked about that encounter for hours afterward.

They stopped in Wellington next, soon after they crossed into Kansas, but there was no sign that the Langer gang had ever stopped there. The next day they headed toward Wichita.

"They're haulin' ass," Shaye said the morning they broke camp to head toward Wichita. "Means they're likely to be late meeting up with Aaron. They're trying to make up for lost time."

"Because of the stop they made in Oklahoma City?" Thomas asked.

"Most likely," Shaye said.

"What about Wichita?" James asked. "Could they be meeting up there?"

"My guess is Wichita's too big," Shaye said. "They'd want something not as busy. My best guess is Salina."

It wasn't that much smaller than Wichita — eleven or twelve hundred people, probably — but it certainly wasn't a place that brought in outsiders. Largely a farming community, it catered mostly to locals, even though the Union Pacific had a stop there. Its claim to fame was the steam-powered wheat mill that was built when wheat began to come into the town in large quantities in the 1870s.

"So should we stop in Wichita?" Thomas asked.

The last good rest they'd had was in Oklahoma City. If the Langers were hauling ass, then Shaye figured they should too, but they might as well ride through Wichita since it would cost them some time to deliberately go around it.

"We could use some coffee," James said after he'd listened to his father's explanation.

"You can hit the general store while I talk

to the local law," Shaye said.

"Do you know who the sheriff is there?" Thomas asked.

"Haven't a clue."

"What if it's someone who . . . you know . . . remembers you?" James asked, worried.

"Statute of limitations ran out on my crimes a long time ago," Shaye said. "Don't worry about it."

All his crimes except one, but he didn't mention that.

Wichita was queen of the cow towns until Dodge City inherited the title in the late 1870s. The cattle drives were now almost over, and even Dodge City's halcyon days were gone.

But Wichita was still a large, bustling place, and impressed Thomas, Matthew, and James, although not as much as Oklahoma City had.

"I only want to be here an hour at the most," Shaye said. "Thomas, you and James go to the general store. Matthew, you come with me."

They all said, "Yes, sir."

Shaye and Matthew rode to the sheriff's office and dismounted in front.

"I'll do all the talking," Shaye said.

"Sure, Pa."

They entered the office and found a tall, slender man with a broom sweeping the floor. Dust was floating in the air, and the sun streaming in the window was reflecting off it. It looked like a man-made dust storm, and Shaye doubted the man was having much effect on the overall cleanliness of the place.

"Excuse me!" he called out.

The man turned abruptly and stopped sweeping. He was possibly the saddest-looking man Shaye had ever seen, and this just from the expression on his face. His mouth curved downward naturally, and the rest of his face seemed to follow. He had no hat on, and had only some wisps of hair left on his head. He appeared to be in his early sixties. Shaye was about to ask for the sheriff when he noticed the badge on the man's chest.

"Are you the sheriff?" he asked.

"Usually," the man said. Gesturing with the broom he added, "Today I'm the janitor too. Just a minute."

The man walked to the corner and set the broom against the wall, then returned to where Shaye and Matthew were standing and extended his hand.

"I'll bet you've swept up a time or two

201

yourself, Sheriff."

"Once or twice."

"Epitaph," the lawman said. "Where is that?"

"South Texas," Shaye said. "Name's Daniel Shaye. This is my son, Matthew."

The sheriff of Wichita reached past Shaye to shake hands with Matthew and said, "Pleased to meet you both. My name's Carmondy, Sheriff Ed Carmondy. What brings you to my neck of the woods, Sheriff? You're a long ways from home."

"Well, I tell you —"

"Have a seat," Carmondy said, cutting him off. "Excuse my bad manners. Get you some coffee?"

"No, thanks," Shaye said.

The sheriff walked around to sit behind his desk. Shaye and Matthew took chairs across from him.

"We're just passing through, trailing a gang that hit the bank in my town and . . . and killed a woman."

"Terrible thing," Carmondy said. "Must have been real bad to bring you all this way on their trail."

"When is killing a woman not terrible?" Shaye asked.

"Too true," Carmondy said. "What can I do to help you?"

"Tell me if there's been any sign of the Langer gang hereabouts in the last day or two."

"Langer gang?"

"Do you know of them?"

"Of course," Carmondy said. "Any lawman worth his salt has heard of the Langers, Ethan and Aaron. Which one you after?"

"Ethan. Aaron and his men robbed a bank in South Dakota about the same time."

"They make that a state yet?" Carmondy asked.

"Think I read something about that in the newspaper some time ago," Shaye said. "Afraid I don't keep up on the new states, though."

"Think we got maybe forty of 'em now," Carmondy said.

"That could be," Shaye said.

"That's a lot of states."

"Sure is."

"You know what town Aaron hit?"

"Heard somewhere near the Bad River — Pierre, maybe."

"Probably a good time to hit that area, what with the statehood stuff goin' on," Carmondy said.

"You could be right," Shaye said. "Sheriff? Any sign of Ethan and his men here?"

"Not that I know of," Carmondy said,

"and I'd know."

"You would?"

"Durn right. I keep my eye out for strangers."

"You do?" Shaye couldn't help himself and looked toward the broom in the corner.

Carmondy smiled, and suddenly his face wasn't so sad anymore. It was an amazing transformation. It seemed whatever his mouth did, the rest of his face followed right along.

"I don't look like much, Sheriff Shaye," he said, "but I know that you rode into town with three deputies, not one."

"Sons," Shaye said. "Three sons, who also happen to be my deputies."

"You must be real proud."

"I am."

Obviously, Sheriff Carmondy was not as dumb as he liked people to think he was.

"So you see, if Ethan Langer rode in with his men — three, four, more — I'd know it."

"I guess you would." Shaye stood up, followed by Matthew. "We won't take up any more of your time, then."

Carmondy stood up and extended his hand. Shaye shook it while Matthew remained behind his father.

"Stayin' in town?" the local lawman asked.

"I know where you and your boys can get a fine meal."

"Thanks, but no," Shaye said. "We've got to keep moving."

"Well, I wish you luck," Carmondy said. "If you track Ethan until he meets up with his brother, you're gonna have a lot to handle, just the four of you."

"We'll make do," Shaye said.

Carmondy looked past Shaye at Matthew and said, "Good luck to you."

Matthew didn't reply, but he touched his hand to the brim of his hat and nodded.

"Matthew," Shaye said outside, "you could have said thank you to the man when he wished you luck."

"But Pa," Matthew said, "you tol' me to let you do all the talkin', didn't you?"

"That I did, son," Shaye said. "That I did."

40

Thomas and James found a good-sized store not far from where they split from Shaye and Matthew, reined their horses in and tied them off out front.

"Coffee," James said, "and some beans."

"And jerky," Thomas said. "Pa gave most of what we had to those Indians."

"That was somethin', wasn't it?" James asked. "The way Pa bargained with them Indians?"

"I'm sure Pa has bargained with Indians before, James," Thomas said. "Just somethin' else we don't know about the man."

"We've found out a bunch of stuff already, Thomas," James said as they stepped up onto the boardwalk. "How much more do you think there is?"

"Lots, James," Thomas said. "I'm sure there's lots."

As they started to enter the store James put his hand on his older brother's arm to stop him.

"Thomas?"

"Yeah?"

"Do you think there's a lot of stuff we don't know about Ma too?" he asked.

"I'll bet there is, James."

"I — I'm not sure I want to know."

"Me neither."

The brothers split up inside the store, which was even larger on the inside than it looked outside. There were several women shopping, and two separate counters with clerks standing at them. One of the clerks was a pretty young woman about James's age, and Thomas allowed his brother to go off in that direction.

"Can I help you with something?" she asked. She smiled at James and completely captivated him.

"Uh, oh, sure, I was, uh, lookin' for some coffee, and some beans. . . ."

"Would you like me to direct you?" she asked. "Or I could show you."

"Maybe you better show me," he said. "This store is pretty big and I, uh, wouldn't want to get lost."

"Certainly."

Thomas thought his brother had recovered nicely after a clumsy start. He decided to step outside and let James do all the shopping.

Out in front of the store, he found a straight-backed wooden chair and sat down with his back to the wall. He watched as the town went by, people going about their daily lives, doing things that he was probably doing weeks ago, before the Langer gang came riding into Epitaph to change his life and the lives of his father and brothers. He wondered if they'd ever get back to leading that kind of carefree life, or if that was all over now. Considering what they were planning on doing, how could they ever go back?

He was still thinking about it when his father and Matthew appeared on horseback before him. He hadn't even noticed them riding up to him. If they'd been someone else entirely, he could have been dead by now. The thought made him shudder.

"Thought you were sleeping," Shaye said, stepping up onto the boardwalk to join him.

"Just thinkin', Pa."

"Where's your brother?"

"He's inside gettin' the supplies," Thomas said. "Found himself a pretty gal to help him."

"You left James alone with a pretty gal?" Matthew asked. "What's he gonna do with his tongue all tied?"

"He was doin' pretty well when I left him."

"I'm gonna go in and have a look," Matthew said.

"I'll wait out here with your brother," Shaye said, slapping Matthew on the back.

"What happened with the local law, Pa?" Thomas asked when his brother went inside.

Briefly, Shaye told him about his conversation with Sheriff Carmondy.

"Do you believe him?"

"I can't start believing that every lawman I talk to is crooked, Thomas," Shaye said. "Or taking money from the Langers."

"But did you believe him?"

"He seems to know what's going on in his own town," Shaye said. "He knew there was four of us here."

"You don't believe him."

"I don't know what to believe," Shaye said. "In order for this gang to operate successfully from Texas to the Dakotas, they've got to have a bunch of lawmen on their payroll."

"How come they didn't try to buy you, Pa?"

"I don't know, Thomas."

"Maybe they heard you were honest?"

"Maybe."

"But wait," Thomas said, "they knew you from the old days."

"If they even knew I was the sheriff of Epitaph," Shaye said. "Who knows? Maybe they came in cold and hit the bank."

"That doesn't sound very professional, does it?"

"No, it doesn't."

"So what are we gonna do?"

"Continue north to Salina, I guess," Shaye said. "Or maybe they'll go west to Hays."

"Wherever they go, Pa," Thomas said, "we'll find them."

Shaye looked down at his son and said, "Yes, we will, Thomas."

Inside the store, James and Matthew had begun elbowing each other for the attention of Janie Summers.

"I'm older," Matthew said.

"I'm smarter," James said.

"I'm bigger."

James thought a moment, then said, "I'm smarter."

"I'm better looking," Matthew said.

Janie laughed and said, "You're both so cute. Will you be staying in town long?"

James and Matthew both pulled long faces, and James said, "We're leavin' as soon as we're done here."

"That's a shame," she said, tallying up their purchases. She'd managed to convince them to buy a few more items than they originally wanted, like a few bars of soap and an extra shirt each. "We could have spent some time . . . talking."

She told them how much their purchases were, and they had to combine their fortunes to pay for it.

"This has been very exciting," she said after they paid her, "meeting two Texas deputies at the same time. Maybe you'll come back this way soon?"

"Maybe," James said, but he doubted it.

"Well, it's been very nice to meet you both," she said, then shook their hands in turn, saying, "James . . . Matthew."

"Nice to meet you too, Miss Janie," Matthew said.

"My Lord," she said as they turned away, "so much excitement in two days. First outlaws, then lawmen."

Both young men stopped and turned back to face her.

"Outlaws?" Matthew asked.

"There were outlaws here yesterday?" James asked.

"Well," Janie said, looking around, her bright blue eyes going wide, "they said they were outlaws, but how was I to know if they were telling the truth? I mean, they couldn't prove it with badges, like you boys could."

"These outlaws," James said, "they didn't happen to say who they were, did they? I mean, who they rode with?"

"Well, there was only two of them," she said, "but they told me they were leading a whole lot more."

"And the name of the gang?" James asked.

"Well," she said, thinking hard, "one of them did say something about being the *segundo* of the Langer gang . . . but he could have been lying. What is a *segundo*, anyway? James? Matthew? Where are you two going?"

41

In their absence, Sheriff Carmondy had once again picked up his broom and was sweeping the floor, raising a hell of a dust cloud again. This time when he turned he saw four men standing in his office — Sheriff Dan Shaye and three other men, no doubt his sons.

"Well," he said, leaning on the broom, "what brings you back so soon?"

Instead of answering, Shaye drew his gun and fired one shot. The bullet sawed clean through the broom handle, and the sheriff went staggering before he caught his balance. The broom ended up on the floor in two pieces.

Carmondy righted himself and threw a look at his gun belt, which was on a hook behind his desk.

"Go ahead," Shaye said. "Go for it, why don't you?"

"Are you crazy?" Carmondy shouted.

213

"What the hell is the matter with you?"

"We just found out that two members of the Langer gang were in town yesterday, buying supplies," Shaye said.

"What? Two of them? Who told you that?"

"The girl at the general store. . . ." Shaye turned to James or Matthew for her name.

"Janie . . ." Matthew said.

"Summers."

"Janie!" Carmondy said. "That gal makes up more stories —"

"Where would she get the word *segundo* from?" Shaye demanded.

"What?"

"She said one of the men claimed to be the *segundo* of the Langer gang."

"I don't . . . she could have heard that word anywhere. Why would a member of the gang announce himself to her?"

"She's a pretty little thing," Shaye said. "Seems to me she'd have men trying to impress her all the time." He turned a glance at his two sons again. "Maybe even getting them to buy things they don't need. Maybe even getting them to brag a bit? Especially if they weren't staying in town long."

"Look, Shaye," Carmondy said, "if two members of that gang were in town yesterday, I didn't know about it."

214

"Come on, now, Sheriff," Shaye said. He took a moment to eject the spent round from his gun, allowing it to fall to the floor. Carmondy watched as he thumbed a live round into the empty chamber. "You know everything there is to know in this town. That's what you told us, anyway."

Carmondy laughed nervously. "I just happened to see you and your boys ride into town, Shaye, that's all," he confessed. "Believe me, fellas ride into town all the time without me knowin' about it."

"So you didn't take any money from Ethan Langer to look the other way?"

"N-No."

"Maybe to lie to any lawmen who might be looking for them?"

"I told you, n-no. I never saw Ethan Langer."

"Or one of his men?" Shaye asked. "Like maybe . . . his *segundo*?"

"What's a *segundo*?" Matthew asked Thomas under his breath.

"I'll tell you later."

"Look, Shaye," Carmondy said, holding both hands out in front of him, "if I knew that the Langer gang was here yesterday, I woulda told you. I swear."

"Want me to whomp him, Pa?" Matthew asked, taking a menacing step toward the

215

local lawman.

"Keep him away!" the man said. "Look, Shaye, I ain't that brave, you know? I wouldn't lie to you. I know your reputation around here."

"My reputation?"

"Well . . . you are Shay Daniels, ain'tcha?"

Shaye stared at the sheriff, then holstered his gun and said, "I used to be."

42

Shaye left the sheriff's office with his three sons following him.

"Why are we leavin', Pa?" Matthew asked.

"I don't think he was lying," Shaye said. "He didn't know that Langer had sent two of the gang into town for supplies."

"How can you be sure?" James asked.

"I'm not," Shaye said, "I just think he's right. He's not that brave — especially if he thought I was still . . . Shaye Daniels."

"So what do we do, Pa?" Matthew asked.

"We're just going to keep going the way we've been going, Matthew. Keep heading north."

They had ridden their horses over to the office, and now they stepped into the street and mounted up.

"Say, James," he said when they were mounted, "did that girl tell you what they bought?"

"No, Pa," James said. "I didn't even think to ask."

"Me neither," Matthew said.

"Well," Shaye said, "let's go and ask her now, shall we?"

James and Matthew argued about who should go back into the store and talk to Janie. Shaye finally told Thomas to dismount and do it.

"I bet he comes out with a bar of soap," James said.

"You and your brother are going to use that soap," Shaye warned him.

"Aw, Pa —" Matthew said.

"You bought it, you're going to use it."

Matthew sulked and James smirked.

"What are you smiling at?" Shaye asked. "That girl bamboozled both of you into buying things you didn't need. You shouldn't be looking so pleased with yourself."

Thomas came walking out empty-handed, looking proud of himself. He mounted up and looked at Shaye.

"Can't blame the boys for buyin' that stuff, Pa," he said. "That one's a charmer."

"Didn't charm you, though, huh?" Shaye asked.

"Not that she didn't try."

"Did you find out what those two Langer

218

men bought?"

"They pretty much did like we did," Thomas said. "Some coffee and jerky, enough for a dozen men or more, but nothin' big."

"That's because they haven't got far to go," Shaye said. "We're getting closer to our destination. Maybe even another couple of days."

"Finally," Thomas said.

"I can't wait," James said.

Matthew remained silent. Shaye knew there was still some doubt going on inside his middle son. They'd all have to keep their promise to talk to him over the next couple of days. If he wasn't totally convinced about what they were doing, Shaye was not going to let him face the Langer gang.

"Let's get going," he said to his sons. "I want to put some miles between us and here before nightfall."

That night they camped in a clearing about sixty miles south of Salina. Shaye waited until they were all gathered around the fire, eating, before discussing their course of action.

"We can make Salina by nightfall tomorrow," he said, "and then one of us has to go in and see if the gang is there. I can't do it, because both Langers might recognize me. One of you has to do it, and I'm going to let the three of you decide which one."

"I'll go," Matthew said right away.

"No, I'll go," James said. "You're too unsure about this, Matthew. Besides, you're so big they'd notice you right away. I can blend in better."

"I'll go," Thomas said.

"Why you?" James demanded.

"I'm the oldest."

"That's got nothin' to do with it," James said, then looked at Shaye and asked, "Does it, Pa?"

"I said I was letting you three decide."

"James's argument about you is a good one, Matthew," Thomas said. "You're too noticeable."

"And what about me?" James asked.

"You're too young."

"You can't pull that on me, Thomas," James said. "I got just as much right to go in as you have. We can both blend in."

"I'm better with a gun, James," Thomas said. "Somethin' might happen, and I'm better equipped to handle it than you."

James opened his mouth to argue, but his argument got trapped in his throat. He looked down at the gun in his holster. He knew he couldn't best Thomas with a gun.

"Sounds like you boys have made up your mind," Shaye said. "Thomas, your brothers and I will camp outside of Salina tomorrow night. You go in, get a hotel room, and have a look around. If the gang — both parts of it — are there, they won't be hard to see." Shaye leaned forward and stared directly at his oldest son. "This is important — do not engage them. Do you understand?"

"I'm not that foolish, Pa," Thomas said. "I wouldn't try to take them alone."

"That's good," Shaye said, "because it's going to be hard enough for just the four of us to do it."

"Don't worry," Thomas said. "If they're in Salina, I'll come back and tell you."

"All right, then," Shaye said. "It's settled."

"What if they're not there, Pa?" James asked.

"We'll cross that bridge when we come to it, James. Let's just take it one step at a time."

Shaye set the watches and gave Matthew the first. While Thomas and James turned in, though, he went and sat next to Matthew.

"Mind if I have a last cup of coffee with you?" he asked.

"Sure, Pa. I'll get it for ya."

221

Matthew poured a cup full and handed it to his father, then poured one for himself.

"You don't really want coffee, do ya, Pa?"

"No, Matthew," Shaye said. "Pretty smart of you to know that."

"I'm not as smart as Thomas and James, Pa, or you," Matthew said, "but I ain't dumb."

"I never thought you were, Matthew. You have something you want to ask me, son?"

"Why ain't I as sure about this as you and Thomas and James, Pa?" Matthew said.

"What part of it is bothering you?"

"Well . . . the God part. You and Thomas are actin' like there ain't no God, and James don't seem so sure anymore."

"And you are?" Shaye asked. "Sure, I mean, about there being a God?"

"If there ain't no God, Pa," Matthew said, "then Ma was lyin' to us all them years that she was takin' us to church."

"And you don't want to think of your mother as a liar, do you, Matthew?"

"No, I don't," Matthew said, "but there's more to it than that. I mean, if what you say about us maybe committin' murder, then it's gonna be a sin."

"A big sin, Matthew."

"And that don't seem to bother you and James and Thomas."

"It bothers you?"

"It's like the biggest mortal sin of all, Pa!"

"I know, son."

"We'll all go to Hell!"

"You have to understand something, Matthew," Shaye said. "I would chase these men through the fires of Hell and out again to get them for what they did to your ma. I don't care if I spend the rest of eternity in Hell, as long as they pay."

Matthew stared at his father with his mouth open. "Wow. Do you think James and Thomas feel that way, Pa?"

Shaye stole a look at his two sleeping sons and said, "Yeah, I think they do."

"Then I should too."

"You don't have to feel that way, Matthew."

"But if I don't, then it means I didn't love her as much as the three of you did."

"It doesn't mean that at all," Shaye said. "It just means you're not ready to give up on God."

"So I gotta choose between Ma and God?"

"You have to choose what's right for you, Matthew," Shaye said. "Nobody else matters."

Matthew looked surprised again. "God don't matter?"

"Not this time, Matthew," Shaye said, putting his hand on his son's shoulder. "Right now the most important is you. All you've got to do is give it some thought, and the answer will come to you."

Shaye dumped the remnants of the coffee into the fire and stood up. "Wake James for the second watch in two hours."

"Yes, Pa."

"Good night, son."

" 'Night, Pa."

Shaye went to his bedroll totally unsure about whether he'd said the right thing to Matthew. These were the times, he knew, when he was going to miss Mary the most.

43

Twenty miles north of Salina, Aaron Langer sat at his campfire while his eleven men sat around their own. Even his longtime *segundo,* Esteban Morales, was not allowed at his fire without an invitation. Next to him he had the saddlebags with the money from the Pierre bank. The ride here from the Bad River in South Dakota had been uneventful for him and his gang, and unlike his brother, he had no trouble sleeping. Killing did not haunt Aaron Langer, it didn't matter if it was man, woman, child, or dog. If they got in his way, they deserved killing.

He turned and looked over his shoulder at the men around the other fire. That was all the signal Morales needed to stand up and come walking over, carrying his plate of beans and bacon.

"Hunker down, Esteban," Aaron said.

"Gracias, Jefe."

"We'll be ridin' into Salina tomorrow."

"All of us, *Jefe*?"

"Yeah, all of us," Aaron said. "With a show of force like we got, nobody's gonna bother us, not even the local law. And once Ethan arrives, we'll have the town under our thumb, if we want it."

"And do we want it?"

"I don't know yet," Aaron said. "We'll have a look around. If the bank looks good, maybe we'll take it."

"We don' usually do that when we meet Ethan in a town," Morales pointed out.

"I know that," Aaron said. "Maybe it's time we did. It would add to our take."

Morales shrugged. Whatever his boss wanted to do was all right with him. Morales had a lot of money put away in a bank in Sonora because he never argued with Aaron Langer. He was also still alive because he never argued.

"*Sí, Jefe,*" he said. "Whatever you say."

"Damn right," Aaron said. "Damn right."

Even his stupid younger brother would never argue with him. Morales had the feeling that if Ethan ever did argue, Aaron wouldn't hesitate to kill his own brother. *Chinga,* for two brothers who had a priest for a third brother, they were both crazy!

"Go on back, Esteban," Aaron said. "I want to be alone to think about tomorrow."

"Bueno," Morales said, and returned to the other fire.

"What'd he have to say, Esteban?" Greg Walters asked.

"Yeah," John Diehl said, "what's the crazy bastard up to now?"

"If he ever heard you call him that, he would kill you," Morales said. "In fact, if I ever hear you call him that again, I will kill you myself."

"Take it easy, Morales," Diehl said. "I was just funnin'."

"Esteban?" Walters said.

"We are all riding into Salina tomorrow," the Mexican said.

"All of us?"

"Sí."

"We're gonna be pretty noticeable," July Edwards said.

"Sí," Morales said. "That does not seem to matter so much to *el jefe.*"

"I guess not," Diehl said.

"What about Ethan?" Walters asked. "If he's there too, with his men, we're gonna make a big crowd."

Morales shrugged. "Whatever he wants, that's what we do," he said, jerking his head toward Aaron Langer. "That is how it has always been, and that is how it will be."

227

The other men fell away into groups while Walters moved over closer to Morales.

"Is he plannin' somethin' crazy, pardner?"

Morales gave Walters a baleful look and asked, "Isn't he always?"

Thirty miles south of Salina, Ethan Langer and his men were camped for the night.

"We're gonna push tomorrow and get to Salina by afternoon," Ethan said. "I don't want Aaron and his men gettin' there much earlier than we do."

The other men nodded, and Ben Branch said, "Okay, Ethan."

Branch was feeling bad about the bragging he'd done to that pretty little gal at the general store in Wichita. If word ever got back to Ethan about that, he knew he'd be dead. The man who had been with him, Larry Keller, hadn't heard him, so he figured he was pretty safe. Wasn't exactly the kind of thing a new *segundo* should be doing.

"If we get to Salina at the same time as Aaron, we're gonna attract a lot of attention, Ethan," Red Hackett said.

"So what?"

"We ain't wanted in Kansas, Red," Branch said.

"That don't matter," Ethan said. "Me and

Aaron, we go where we want, when we want. Don't matter if we're wanted." He looked around at his men. "Anybody don't want to go to Salina tomorrow? Let me know now and you'll give up your share. Anybody? No? Then shut the hell up for the rest of the night. I'll kill the next man who asks me a question. Got it?"

They all got it, and didn't say a word.

The next morning three separate groups of riders began to make their way toward the town of Salina, Kansas.

44

Aaron Langer and his men were the first to arrive in Salina. Riding in *en masse,* they attracted as much attention as they thought they would.

Watching them ride by from his window, Sheriff Matt Holcomb turned and said to his deputy, Ray Winston, "Ray, go and find Zeke and Will. I want all three of you here in half an hour."

"What's goin' on, Sheriff?"

"Trouble just rode into town," Sheriff Holcomb said, "in bunches."

Holcomb didn't recognize Aaron Langer as he led his men into town, but he did recognize trouble when he saw it, and these men were it.

There were several hotels in Salina, and some boardinghouses. The strangers had put their horses up at the livery and then split up, some to hotels, some to boarding-houses. Holcomb figured their leader was smart enough to keep them all from staying in one place.

"Have a seat," he told his three deputies when they got back.

"What's this is all about, Sheriff?" Zeke Abbott asked.

"A bunch of strangers rode into town today," Holcomb said. "I didn't like the look of them."

"Why do you think they're here?" Will Strunk asked.

"Trouble."

"Like what?"

"The bank maybe," Holcomb said. "We're gonna keep an eye on the bank."

Zeke swallowed and asked, "How many of them were there?"

"Maybe a dozen."

"A dozen?" Will asked. "Like twelve?"

"That's right."

"Against the four of us?" Zeke asked.

"Relax," Holcomb said. "Maybe I'm wrong. For now, we're just gonna keep an eye on the bank, and on them."

"Sheriff," Zeke said, "it sounds to me like we need more men."

"If we need them, we'll get them, Zeke," Holcomb said. "For now, just do as you're told and we'll be fine."

Zeke wasn't seeing it that way. He stood

up, took off his badge, and put it on the desk.

"I can't do this," he said. "This is supposed to be a quiet town. That's the only reason I took this job six months ago."

"It's been a quiet town, Zeke," Holcomb said. "Do you mean that at the first sign of trouble you're just gonna quit?"

"That's exactly what I'm gonna do," Zeke said. "Sorry, Sheriff."

As he went out the door, the sheriff faced his other two deputies.

"What about you fellas?" he asked. "Are you gonna quit too?"

"I'm not quittin'," Ray Winston said.

"Me neither," Will Strunk said.

"Well . . . good," Holcomb said. "Now we just need to decide who watches the bank and who watches the leader of those men . . . whoever he is."

Zeke Abbott left the sheriff's office and crossed the street to the Somerset Saloon. Inside, he found Aaron Langer seated with a few of his men. There were no other patrons in the place, since they had vacated at the first sign of the outlaws. The bartender and owner, Sam Somerset, stood behind the bar, wiping the top with a rag. He was afraid to stay, but afraid to leave.

"Zeke," Aaron Langer said. "What's the good word?"

"The sheriff and two deputies," Zeke said. "That's it, Mr. Langer."

"Good job," Langer said. "Have a drink. Bartender, give the ex-deputy a beer, on me."

"Yes, sir."

Langer laughed, looked at his men and said, "Put in on my bill."

"Yes, sir."

45

Aaron Langer put two men outside the saloon in chairs, keeping watch on the street. When those men noticed the deputy across the street, one of them got up and moseyed back inside.

"Lawman across the street," he said to Aaron.

"That don't matter," Aaron said, looking up from his whiskey. "They're just keepin' an eye on us. According to Zeke, there's one sheriff and only two deputies. You stay outside with Rafe and watch for my brother."

"Right."

That man went back outside. Aaron turned his head, looked around and settled on another. "Tate!"

"Yeah, boss."

"Take a walk around town, see if you spot the other two lawmen anywhere."

"Yeah, boss."

"And take somebody with you." He turned back around. "I don't want any of us caught alone."

"Right, boss." Tate reached out and tapped another man on the shoulder. The man followed him outside.

Esteban Morales, seated across from Aaron, took the whole thing in but said nothing. He doubted the law would take any action unless they did first. This put his boss, Aaron Langer, firmly in control, which suited him just fine.

Sheriff Holcomb had put Ray Winston across from the saloon and Will Strunk across from the bank. He made rounds, checking both locations out. He was down the street from the bank when he saw the two strangers coming from the other direction. Across the street, standing in a doorway, smoking a quirly, was his deputy. Blowing smoke that way was a sure way to get noticed. Both his deputies were young — ten to twelve years younger than his own thirty-six — and would have to be told.

He claimed a doorway for himself and watched the strangers. They didn't seem interested in the bank. Most of their attention was on the deputy. They watched him for a few moments, and Holcomb didn't think Deputy Strunk was even aware they were there. After those few moments, they turned and headed back the other way — he assumed, to report back to their boss. Aaron Langer was clearly checking out the town and counting lawmen.

When the men were gone, Holcomb crossed the street to bawl out his deputy.

Thomas came up to Shaye's side when they had only been riding about two hours.

"Pa?"

"Yes, Thomas?"

"I think I can make better time alone, pushing my horse," he said.

"You're probably right, Thomas."

"I'd be able to check out Salina in the daylight."

Shaye gave it some thought. "You'll have to be careful, Thomas."

"I won't make a move on them," Thomas said, "and they won't recognize me —"

"That's not what I mean. There's going to be a lot of strangers in town. The law will assume that you're with them."

"I'll have my badge," Thomas said. "I won't wear it into town, but I'll go and see the local law and introduce myself."

"All right," Shaye said. "You seem to have thought this out."

236

"I have."

"Give your bag of supplies to one of your brothers, then, and go ahead. We'll still stop just outside of town — about a mile or two due south — and wait to hear from you."

"Yes, Pa."

"If we don't hear something from you tonight, we'll come on in."

"I'll get back to you tonight, Pa."

"You'd better, son," Shaye said. "You'd better."

46

Several hours after the arrival of Aaron Langer and his gang, Sheriff Holcomb had schooled both of his deputies and hoped they would now be a little less conspicuous. He, himself, had taken a chair from his office and was sitting out front watching the street. That's where he was when the second set of strangers rode in.

Ethan Langer noticed the sheriff sitting in front of his office, and had the gall to tip his hat to the man.

"Where are we supposed to meet Aaron?" Ben Branch asked.

"In a saloon, where else?" Ethan answered.

"Which one?"

"I don't know," Ethan said. "Why don't we try one with a deputy across the street from it."

That turned out to be a good plan. They saw the deputy standing in the doorway across from the Somerset Saloon and reined in their horses in front of it. They also saw two men sitting in front of the saloon.

"Did you see the lawman across from the bank?" Branch asked Ethan.

"I saw him," Ethan said. "The one in front of the office is the sheriff. The other two are deputies."

"Think that's all there are?"

"I don't know," Ethan said, "but assuming Aaron got here before us, he'll know. You know the two men sitting out front?"

Branch took a look, then said, "I think one of them is Rafe Simpson."

Ethan knew the name. "Okay, then," he said. "Aaron's here. Have two of our men take the horses over to the livery."

"Right."

"I'll meet you inside."

Ethan dismounted and entered the saloon without looking over at the two men.

"Asshole," Rafe Simpson said under his breath.

"Don't ever let Aaron hear you say that," the other man warned.

"He says it himself."

"It's his brother."

When Ben Branch stepped up onto the boardwalk, Rafe stood up and said,

"Branch, ain't it?"

"That's right, Rafe."

The two men shook hands.

"You look short," Rafe said, eyeing the men behind Branch. "Where's Petry?"

"Dead."

Rafe looked surprised. "He get hit when you took the bank?"

"No," Branch said, "Ethan killed him."

Rafe looked even more surprised. "Who's *segundo*?"

"Me," Branch said, "and it ain't a job I ever wanted."

"I don't blame you," Rafe said. "Goin' inside for a drink?"

Branch hesitated, then said, "I think I'll give Ethan a coupla minutes with his brother."

Rafe grinned and said, "Don't blame you for that either."

When Ethan walked through the door, he spotted Aaron immediately. He ignored his brother's men and walked to the table where Aaron was sitting with his *segundo,* Esteban Morales.

"It's about time, little brother," Aaron said. "We've been here for hours."

"Hey, we're here," Ethan said, tossing his saddlebags onto the table, almost upsetting the bottle of whiskey Aaron had there.

Aaron reached down, lifted his saddlebags from the floor, and deposited them on the table with his brother's.

"Morales, give my brother your chair," he said.

Without a word, Morales stood up and walked away. Instead of joining the men at one of the other tables, he went and stood at the bar.

"Morales!" Aaron called out. "A glass."

The Mexican turned, took a glass from the bartender and tossed it to his boss, who caught it with one hand. Aaron set the glass down and poured it full from the bottle. As Ethan sat, his brother pushed the glass toward him across the table.

"Good to see you, Ethan," Aaron said, lifting his own glass. "You look like shit."

"Good to see you too, Aaron." He lifted his glass, drained it, and slapped it back down on the table.

Ben Branch came in then, leading Ethan's men, followed by Aaron's two who had been sitting outside.

"You look short a man or two," Aaron said.

"I had to kill Petry."

"Had to?"

"No choice," Ethan said.

Aaron accepted his brother's word without asking for an explanation. Once all the men were in the saloon, their total number was nineteen.

"We'll have to get you a couple more men," Aaron said, "to even our number out."

"Whatever," Ethan said. "We don't have to worry about that until tomorrow. What's with the law outside?"

"They're keepin' an eye on us," Aaron said. "Now that you're here, they'll be keepin' an eye on all of us."

"How many?"

"Three."

"Nothin' to worry about?"

"Not a thing."

Ethan scratched his chin, then rubbed his face with both hands. The last couple of nights, the woman had come back in full force, screamin' until he woke up. Last night he had almost put his gun in his mouth and pulled the trigger, but that would have been letting her win.

"Ethan?" Aaron said. "What's wrong?"

"Nothin'," Ethan said. "When are we gonna count?"

Aaron studied his brother and knew something was wrong. Ethan was keeping something from him, and that wouldn't do.

"Later," Aaron said. "Have another drink."
He poured another glass. "Let's talk awhile."
"About what?"
"Let's see what we can come up with."

47

Pushing his horse hard, Thomas Shaye reached Salina one hour after Ethan Langer and his men. He paused just outside of town, his horse blowing beneath him, removed his badge and placed it in his shirt pocket. He gave the horse a few more moments to catch its breath, then started for town at a walk.

Sheriff Holcomb was unhappy with the fact that all the strangers were in the Somerset Saloon and had been there for an hour. But at least they hadn't gone near the bank yet. He knew they had to be planning something, though.

Over the past couple of hours, the traffic had dwindled down until the street was empty. Word had gotten around, and people had taken to the safety of their homes, expecting an explosion. He had two deputies, and at his best count there were at least eighteen gunmen in the saloon — maybe nineteen.

The fella riding down Main Street at the moment could well be making it twenty, but he didn't seem to be in any hurry to do it.

What surprised the lawman about this man was that he rode right up to his office and stopped. Then he reined his horse in and looked down at him.

"Can I help you?" Holcomb said.

"You the sheriff?" the stranger asked.

"That's right." The man dropped his arms to his sides, either to get his hand near his gun or to show off the badge on his chest. "Holcomb's the name."

"My name's Thomas Shaye, Sheriff," Thomas said. He looked up and down the street. "It's real quiet around here."

"A town can generally feel when trouble's a-brewin'," the lawman explained.

"You got trouble here?"

"You mean you don't know?"

"I have an idea."

"Your friends are in the Somerset Saloon," Holcomb said, "if you want to join them."

"How many?"

"Maybe twenty," Holcomb said, "with you."

"Nineteen, then."

"You ain't with them?"

Thomas was still concerned that someone was going to see them. "Can we go in your office and talk?"

"Give me one good reason."

Thomas looked around again, then removed his badge from his pocket and showed it to the sheriff.

"Okay," Holcomb said, getting up from his chair, "that's a good enough reason."

He led the way into his office.

Aaron and Ethan exchanged stories about their bank jobs, and Aaron was quite interested to hear about the woman.

"So you just rode her down?"

"The bitch stepped out in front of us, Aaron," Ethan said. "There wasn't any way to avoid her."

"You never killed a woman before, Ethan," Aaron said. "How'd you take it?"

Ethan snorted and said, "She got what she deserved."

The bags beneath Ethan's eyes told Aaron his younger brother had not been sleeping well. Abruptly, though, he turned his head and shouted at Rafe.

"Get back outside, we'll want to know if that lawman is comin' this way."

"Right, boss."

"Take somebody with you."

"I'll go," Ben Branch said. Grabbing his beer from the bar, he followed Rafe outside, but they were too late to see Thomas going into the sheriff's office. They both saw the horse in front, but it didn't register with either of them as unusual. They sat down and started exchanging stories about their bosses, ignoring the deputy who was still stationed across the street.

48

"So you've got a posse with you?" Sheriff Holcomb asked Thomas hopefully.

"Not exactly."

"Got one comin' behind you." Holcomb began to pace the length of his office.

"No," Thomas said. "I've got three men waitin' for me just outside of town. My father is the sheriff of Epitaph, me and my brothers are his deputies."

"Sheriff Shaye?" Holcomb asked.

"That's right."

"So there's only four of you?"

"That's right."

"And you're after these two gangs?"

"It's one gang," Thomas said, "run by two brothers."

"Wait a minute." The lawman stopped pacing and faced Thomas. "Are we talkin' about . . . the Langer gang?"

"That's right."

"Oh my God," Holcomb said. "I should

have guessed. The leader of the first group . . . he must have been Aaron."

"I guess," Thomas said. "We've been trailing Ethan Langer and his men."

"All the way from Texas?" Holcomb asked. "Because of a . . . a bank job?"

"Not just a bank robbery," Thomas said. "They killed a woman . . . my mother."

"Oh," Holcomb said. "Well . . . I guess that's worth travelin' all this way."

"Are they all here?"

"I guess," Holcomb replied. "Like I said, eighteen, maybe nineteen. How many hit your bank?"

"About eight, maybe nine."

"So four of you tracking eight. I guess the odds didn't seem so bad then."

"How many deputies have you got?"

"Two."

"So now it's seven against nineteen," Thomas said.

"Not so good, eh?"

"I guess not," Thomas said with a shrug, "but we've got somethin' they don't."

"What's that?"

"My pa."

49

James came up next to Shaye and handed him a cup of coffee. "Worried about Thomas, Pa?"

"Yeah, I am, James."

They had camped about half an hour before, and James was making them something to eat. The coffee was ready first. They'd made good time and had managed to camp before dark.

Shaye was standing away from the fire, looking off in the direction of town.

"He'll be okay, Pa," James said. "Thomas is smart."

"Yes, he is."

"And he's good with a gun."

Shaye turned to look at his youngest son. "He's good at shooting at tin cans and bottles, James," he said, "and varmints. He's never had to face another man with a gun. None of you has."

"But we're gonna have to, ain't we?"

"Yes," Shaye said, "yes, it's unavoidable . . . unless we just quit and go back."

"We can't do that, Pa," James said. "Not after what they did to Ma. We can't! Matthew and Thomas, they'll tell you the same thing."

Shaye hesitated a moment, then said, "Yeah, I know they would."

"Pa," James said, "you told us we couldn't think about this too much. Don't you start doing it."

"You're right, James," Shaye said. "Thank you."

"I better get the food ready," James said. "Matthew'll just burn it all up."

"Okay."

James went back to the fire, and Shaye went back to staring off into the distance, waiting for some sign of Thomas.

"So what do you plan to do?" Holcomb asked, looking out his window. It was starting to get dark.

"I have to ride out and get my pa and my brothers," Thomas said. "We'll come back under cover of darkness."

"And then what?"

"Then it's up to you and my pa," Thomas said. "You're in charge here, but I think if you listen to my pa, everything'll go okay."

Holcomb hesitated.

"They probably won't do anythin' to-night," Thomas said. "We'll be back in a couple of hours."

"All right," Holcomb said. "I'll wait here."

"Pull your men in," Thomas suggested.

"Why?"

"It'll make them think they're in the clear. Give them a false sense of security."

"A false sense of security?" Holcomb asked. "With their numbers, I don't think it's so false."

"My pa will figure out somethin', Sheriff," Thomas said. "Just pull your men in and wait for us here."

"Okay, Deputy," Holcomb said, "okay. We'll wait for you and your father and your brothers here, but I hope you're right about your father comin' up with somethin'."

"Don't worry, Sheriff," Thomas said, "he will."

Shaye was the first one to hear the horse, and he looked up from his plate.

"It's Thomas, Pa!" Matthew said.

Both James and Matthew started to rise but Shaye waved them down and stood himself, his hand on his gun.

"Let's make sure," he said. "Just be still."

They both settled back down, their hands

252

on their guns, like their father. The sound of the horse came closer, and then Thomas came bursting into the light of their campfire, his horse kicking up dust as he reined it in.

"They're there, Pa!" he said excitedly. "They're all there."

James and Matthew jumped up and joined their father in rushing to Thomas's side.

"Calm down, Thomas," Shaye said, "and tell me everything."

50

"What are we waitin' for, Aaron?" Ethan demanded after his brother had kept him talking for hours. The other men in the saloon were wondering the same thing. "Let's compare our hauls and get the split done."

Ethan reached for the saddlebags, but Aaron slammed a big hand down on them.

"We'll do the tally and the split when I say so," he hissed at his brother. "You've got somethin' on your mind, somethin' botherin' you, and I wanna know what it is!"

They had finished the bottle of whiskey and started on another one. Morales was the only one in the room who knew that the brothers' capacity for liquor knew no bounds. The others thought the two of them would get so drunk they wouldn't be able to tally until tomorrow. In fact, Branch had sent one of Ethan's men out to get them hotel rooms. Now it was pitch-black out and they were all still there, with two men sitting outside.

At least, the deputy on watch across the street had been pulled off, Morales thought. Now the brothers had their heads together across the table and no one could hear them.

"Tell me what's botherin' you, Ethan," Aaron said. "You look like you ain't slept in days."

Ethan tried to match his brother's glare, but as usual, he was unable to. "Aaron —"

"We ain't leavin' this saloon tonight until I find out what's goin' on," Aaron said. "You killed Petry! That's crazy. What else have you done?"

Ethan stared at Aaron, wet his lips and said, "I went to see Vincent."

"So you got the sheriff to pull his men in and wait?" Shaye asked. "That was good work."

"It wasn't hard, Pa," Thomas said. "He really doesn't know what to do."

They had listened to what Thomas had to say and then broke camp and headed for Salina. Shaye was riding alongside Thomas, with James and Matthew behind them.

"He's only got two deputies."

"Maybe he can round up some more men when we get there," Shaye said.

"Yeah," James said from behind him, "maybe the people in Salina care more than the people in Epitaph did."

Shaye found that a remarkably bitter statement to be coming from his youngest son.

"I guess we'll find out when we get there," he said.

They rode into town as quietly as they could, with Thomas leading them around back behind the sheriff's office. They dismounted and knocked on the back door.

One of the deputies let them in. "This way," he said, and led them through the cell block to the office, where two more men with badges were waiting for them.

"Sheriff," Thomas said, "this is my father, Sheriff Shaye. Pa, that's Sheriff Holcomb."

Holcomb came across the room to shake hands with Shaye. "Pleased to meet you," he said. "Your son seems to have a lot of faith in you."

"Well," Shaye said, "I hope it's well-placed."

"So do I," Sheriff Holcomb said. "These are my deputies, Ray and Will."

"My other sons, James and Matthew."

The men shook hands all around.

"Are they still in the saloon?" Shaye asked.

"The saloon's down the street but you can see it from here," Holcomb said, moving to the window. "They haven't moved."

"You'd think they'd have done their tally and split by now," Shaye said, standing beside Holcomb and peering out. "Is there a back way in?"

"Yeah."

"It's dark," Shaye said, "but looks like they have two men sitting out front."

"Ever since they got here," Holcomb said, "except for when your boy rode into town."

Shaye turned away from the window.

"How do you want to play this?" Holcomb asked.

"It's your town," Shaye said. "Can you get some more men?"

"This time of night I'd say no," Holcomb said. "Actually, any time of day I'd say no. The whole town knows that these men rode in today, and they got off the streets fast."

"So they figure this is your job, huh?"

"That's right."

"What do we do, Pa?" Matthew asked.

"Making a move at night could be good for us, Pa," Thomas said. "We can use the dark."

"Anybody else got any ideas?" Shaye asked.

"Your boy here said you'd know what to

257

do, Sheriff Shaye," Holcomb said, and then stopped and stared at Shaye for a moment. "Wait a minute."

"What is it?" Shaye asked, but he thought he knew.

"Shaye?"

"That's right."

"Aren't you . . . Shay Daniels?"

"It's Sheriff Dan Shaye."

"I know you!"

"Sheriff —"

"Shay Daniels!" Holcomb turned to his two deputies. "You fellas know the name Shay Daniels, right?"

"Sounds familiar," Will said, but Ray shook his head and asked, "Who is he?"

"He's Shay Daniels," Holcomb said, looking back at Shaye.

"Sheriff," Shaye said, "there was a time in my life when that was my name, but that really doesn't matter now, does it?"

"It sure does," Holcomb said. "I wasn't sure what your boy meant when he said we had somethin' they didn't — meanin' you — but now I do." He turned and looked at his deputies. "Boys, we got a real Kansas legend on our hands, here. Back in the seventies there wasn't no one quicker with a gun in these parts — hell, Missouri neither — than Shay Daniels."

Thomas, James, and Matthew stared at their father. If what Sheriff Holcomb was saying was true, then he hadn't been quite as truthful with them as he indicated.

"Now, wait," Shaye said, "that stuff is just reputation. You can't believe everything you hear —"

"I saw you!" Holcomb said suddenly, pointing at Shaye. "I just remembered, I saw you in St. Joe. You outdrew three men in the street, and they was pretty good gun hands. Wait, I'll remember who they were. . . ."

"Never happened," Shaye said. "You're mixing me up with someone else, or you're remembering wrong. Can we get back to what we're supposed to be doing here?"

"Okay," Holcomb said, "but it'll come to me. Okay, you take the lead, Daniels, and we'll follow."

"It's Dan," Shaye said, "or Sheriff. Don't call me Daniels!"

His three sons were shocked at their father's vehemence, as were the local lawmen.

"Okay, okay," Holcomb said, moving his hands in a placating gesture. "Sorry. But you call the tune . . . Sheriff Shaye . . . and we'll dance to it."

51

"A dream?" Aaron asked.

"That's right."

"A bad dream?"

"Yeah."

Ethan was waiting for the humiliation. The sooner it started, the sooner it would be over and they could get to the tally.

"About the woman?"

"Yeah, Aaron," Ethan said, "about the woman."

"What is she doin'?" Aaron asked. "In the dream, I mean."

"Screamin'."

Aaron sat back and stared across the table at his brother. The others in the room drank, or ate, or sighed, or just plain waited. No one had the nerve to ask any questions.

Ethan sat and waited for his brother's abuse.

"And you thought you could talk to Vincent about this, and not me?" Aaron asked.

"Uh . . ." This was not the question Ethan had anticipated. He'd expected a lot of others, but not that one.

Aaron looked around the room, and everyone he looked at contrived to be looking somewhere else.

"Morales!"

Morales came over, carrying a beer. *"Jefe"*?

"Keep everyone here," Aaron said. "My brother and I are gonna go and talk in a room upstairs."

"Should I hold onto the money?" Morales asked.

"No," Aaron said, "we'll be taking that with us. I just don't want anyone goin' anywhere. Understand?"

"Sí."

Ethan didn't understand, but he never questioned his brother either — not when he was looking this serious.

"Branch?"

"Yeah, boss."

Ethan turned his head and looked at his *segundo,* leaning against the bar. "Come over here."

"Oh, sure boss." Branch came over.

"Aaron and I are goin' to a room upstairs to talk," Ethan said. "Keep the men here."

"Right. Gonna do the tally upstairs?"

Ethan ignored the question. "Just keep

261

everyone here."

"Okay, boss."

Aaron and Ethan picked up their saddle-bags and went upstairs to look over the rooms.

"First," Shaye said to Holcomb, "do you have any more deputy badges?"

"Two more."

"Give them to two of my sons," Shaye said.

"What for?"

"Cover," Shaye said, "in case they're seen. I don't want them walking around with Texas badges on."

Holcomb handed two of his badges to James and Matthew, who removed theirs and replaced them with the local ones. They put their own badges in their shirt pockets. Thomas had removed his earlier, and Shaye removed his now.

"Now what?" Holcomb asked.

"We should make a move while they're all in one place," Shaye said. "If we do this right, we should be able to get the drop on them and surround them."

"The seven of us," Holcomb asked, "surround nineteen men?"

"It can be done," Shaye said. "We just have to time it right. Have your deputies used their guns?"

"Yes."

"On other men?"

"A time or two, yes," Holcomb said.

"Killed anyone?"

"No."

"Okay," Shaye said, "my boys haven't either, so this might be a first for them."

"Not for me," the sheriff said, "or you either."

"No."

They both looked at the other young men in the room.

"Is everybody ready for this?" Holcomb asked.

"I'm ready," Will said.

"Me too," Ray echoed.

"Your boys?" Holcomb asked Shaye.

"I don't have to ask them," Shaye said. "They're ready."

"So how do we go about this?"

"Tell me about the saloon," Shaye said. "You already told me about the back door. What other ways in and out . . ."

When they chose a room with a couple of poker tables instead of beds, Ethan closed the door, turned and walked into his brother's right fist. He went flying over one of the tables, his saddlebags of cash falling to the floor. Aaron picked them up and tossed them onto the other table with his bags, then walked over to his fallen brother.

"Wha—" Ethan said, but Aaron didn't let him get the question out. He hauled him to his feet and held him there a moment.

"That was for pickin' Vincent over me," he said.

"Aaron —"

His brother silenced him by hitting him again, but he held the front of his shirt with his other hand to keep him from falling.

"That's for killin' that woman when you didn't have to," he said. "You'll probably bring a posse down on us for that."

"I didn't —"

Aaron hit him again, and let him fall. When Ethan hit the floor, he lay still, but was still conscious.

"And that's for bein' a damned baby about killin' the woman and havin' bad dreams about it," Aaron said, leaning over Ethan. "I should hit you twice for that, but I'm lumpin' them together."

Ethan's eyes fluttered but stayed open. Eventually he focused on Aaron's face.

"Did you hear me?" Aaron asked.

"I heard you," Ethan said. He extended his arm. "Help me up, damn it."

Aaron reached down, grabbed his brother's hand, and pulled him to his feet. As Ethan came up, he balled up his left fist and hit Aaron in the face with it.

Downstairs, the men heard the commotion above them, and looked at Morales and Branch to see if they should do anything. Both men simply stood at the bar drinking their beer.

"Think Ethan is fightin' back?" Branch asked.

Morales swallowed the last of his beer before answering, put the mug on the bar for the bartender to refill. "If he is, it'll be the first time in his life."

"Would Aaron kill him for that?"

Morales accepted the full mug from the barman and drank a third of it before answering.

"He would probably respect him for it," he said, "and that would also be a first."

52

The seven men left the sheriff's office by the back door. Shaye and his sons were armed with rifles they'd removed from their saddles. The local lawmen had shotguns from the office gun rack. Thomas went with Sheriff Holcomb to take care of the two men who were still sitting out in front of the saloon. Deputy Ray Winston paired up with Matthew to go around to the back door and get into the saloon that way. Deputy Will Strunk and James were going to go around to one side of the saloon and get in through a window, while Shaye went alone to the other side to do the same.

Thomas had to go completely around the building to come at the two men in front of the saloon without being seen by them. The sheriff, who would approach them more directly, gave him five minutes to do that. Thomas actually passed his brother and Will Strunk while they were working on a first floor window.

When he got to his assigned spot, he was able to see the sheriff approaching from the other side. The men there were supposed to be on watch, but they weren't watching very well. From what Thomas could hear, they were bitching that they'd had to sit inside or outside this saloon all day long, and what the hell was the matter with those two damned brothers?

The sheriff sidled up on them before they knew it and spoke to them, getting their attention.

"Nice night to be sittin' outside, ain't it?"

Both men, startled, began to go for their guns.

"I wouldn't do that," Thomas said from behind them.

Both men froze. Thomas already had his gun out, and now Holcomb produced his.

"You fellas don't know what you're doin'," one of the men said.

"Hopefully," Holcomb said, "we'll figure it out along the way. Right now I'm just gonna take your guns, so stand easy so my friend there doesn't have to shoot you."

It was the first time Thomas had ever held his gun on another man.

James and Will Strunk got the window open

and slipped quietly inside the saloon. They found themselves in an office. Outside the office door, they could hear men talking.

Now they just had to wait.

Meanwhile, Matthew and Ray Winston slipped the back door open and entered. They found themselves in a hallway that led to a curtained doorway. Beyond that doorway was the saloon.

Aaron shook off the punch from Ethan, which didn't have much sting behind it, but as Morales had predicted, brought forth a look of respect.

"You ready to tally?" Aaron asked.

Ethan wiped blood from his face with his sleeve and said, "Yeah."

Aaron went outside and shouted downstairs, "Morales and Branch, come on up."

There was a low roof on the other side of the building, and Shaye was able to climb up onto it and gain access to a window. He managed to slide it open and climb in, finding himself in a room with a bed.

He didn't know that in the room right next to him four men were counting money out onto a poker table.

Shaye opened the door to the room as quietly as he could and stepped out. He was on a balcony overlooking the saloon. There were easily a dozen men or more downstairs. He couldn't get a clear count. He hoped the entire gang was all there.

He waited for the first move to be made.

James cracked the door to the office open and peered out. He also could see many men, but could not count. No one had any way of knowing if all the men were present.

He and Will waited.

Matthew and Ray peered through the curtain. They could see plenty of men with guns, but could not get a count. They waited impatiently to make their move.

The first move was to come from Thomas and Sheriff Holcomb. They had relieved the two men of their guns, and now they turned them to face the bat-wing doors. They intended to use their prisoners as cover as they entered the saloon.

"If one of you fellas moves wrong," Holcomb said, "we'll put a bullet in both your backs? Got it?"

"We got it," one of them said, "but you're gonna be sorry. There's a lot of men with guns in there."

"How many men?" Holcomb asked.

"You'll find out."

"If they open fire, you'll be the first to go," Thomas said.

Holcomb looked at Thomas, who nodded and said, "Let's do this."

53

Holcomb and Thomas each pushed their man through the bat-wing doors, then entered right behind them.

"This is the sheriff!" Holcomb shouted. "Keep your hands away from your guns."

The thirteen men in the room froze momentarily. The four men they would have taken orders from were not there. As a result, they had to make their own individual decisions.

At the sound of Holcomb's voice, the others made their moves.

James and Deputy Strunk opened the office door and stepped out, guns in their hands. James's heart was pounding, and he tried to ignore it.

Matthew and Deputy Winston stepped through the curtained doorway with their guns out. Matthew's mouth was dry. He still wasn't sure that he was with his father and brothers on what they were going to do, but this seemed okay to him. After all, they were acting with the local law.

Shaye stood up straight and pointed his gun at the men on the first floor.

"Play it smart and lay down your guns," he called out. "You're surrounded!"

Red Hackett looked up and saw Shaye looking down on them with his gun out. He didn't recognize the man, or any of the others, but he knew two things — they were lawmen, and he and his *compadres* outnumbered them.

"Surrounded, my ass!" he shouted, and went for his gun.

That was all the others needed. They all went for their weapons, and the shooting started. . . .

"What the hell!" Ethan said.

He started for the door with Ben Branch in tow. Morales looked at Aaron, who shook his head. From the sounds outside the room, all hell had broken loose.

"Ethan, wait!" Aaron shouted.

"What for?"

"The law's made their move."

"But there was only supposed to be three of them."

"Sounds like a lot more than that to me,"

272

Aaron said, "and if they got the drop on our men, it's gonna be bad."

"So what do we do?" Ethan asked.

Aaron waved his arm at the stacks of money on the table. "We pack this money up and go out that window," he said. "There's a roof out there. We can make it to the street and get our horses from the livery."

"But —"

"There's a lot of money here," Aaron said, "and a lot more if it's only split four ways."

Ethan hesitated.

"What do we do, Ethan?" Branch asked.

Morales was ready to draw his gun to back Aaron Langer's play. He'd leave Ethan to his own brother, and he would take out Branch, if it came to that.

"Ethan," Aaron said. "What do we do?"

The shooting in the saloon was getting impossibly loud. It sounded like a war.

"Pack it up, Aaron," Ethan finally said, "and let's get the hell out of here."

54

The lawmen were outnumbered, but they had the outlaws outgunned. Holcomb, Strunk, and Winston all let loose with their shotguns, both barrels, and then put their pistols to use. Men cried out and blood splashed onto the bar, the floor, and the walls.

Shaye picked off several men from the balcony with his Winchester — levering and firing, levering and firing — before they knew what hit them.

Matthew and James put their rifles to use from the floor level, then pressed their handguns into action. There was no hesitation from either of them. This was clearly a kill or be killed situation.

Thomas, preferring his handgun to his rifle, used that weapon first, and didn't switch to the rifle until his hammer fell on an empty chamber. Like his brothers, he never hesitated, but unlike them, he was calm, which surprised him. Not only was he calm, but he was deadly accurate, and every bullet he fired slammed into somebody's flesh.

The outlaws were confused, unsure where to shoot first. With no direction, they were easy pickings, even though there were more of them. A couple jumped behind the bar, where the poor bartender was cowering, but they were visible from the balcony and Shaye took care of them.

From his vantage point, Shaye could see his sons in action. As proud of them as he was, he was actually watching to make sure they didn't get hurt. He knew he was making a mistake — possibly a deadly one. In watching out for his sons, he was leaving himself open, but this was the first time they had been involved in a gunfight. If one of them panicked, he wanted to be able to help them.

He saw a bullet strike Will Strunk, who was standing next to James, and the deputy went down. To James's credit, he just kept on shooting.

As Shaye had taught them, his sons went to one knee, or to cover, in order to reload.

In Thomas's case, he upturned a table and ducked behind it.

James dropped to a knee, as did Matthew, but Matthew was still a big target.

Shaye did his best to protect his sons with his rifle, and then with his pistol, until the room filled with so much gun smoke that he couldn't see them.

He was about to rush to the stairs when the shooting abruptly stopped.

His trained ear picked up the sounds of men moaning, empty shells striking the floor as some reloaded, rifle levers being worked and shotguns being broken over to reload.

He didn't wait for the smoke to clear, but headed for the stairs. Halfway down, he was able to see again. He anxiously sought out his sons.

Thomas was standing up behind the table he'd overturned, calmly reloading.

James was crouched over the fallen deputy.

Matthew was still down on one knee, but he held his gun at the ready. Next to him, Deputy Winston was holding his hand over a wound he'd sustained to his arm.

Sheriff Holcomb was moving among the fallen outlaws. There didn't seem to be any left standing, but from the sound they were making, quite a few of them were still alive.

"Pa," Thomas said, still calm, "you're hit."

"What?" Shaye looked down at himself

and saw blood on his side. He hadn't felt it, but a bullet had plowed a furrow in his left side and kept on going. He probed it with his fingers, then looked up at Thomas.

"It's not bad," he said. "The bullet's not there. You boys all right?"

"I'm, fine, Pa," James said, "but the deputy's dead."

"Damn!" Holcomb said.

"Sorry about your man, Sheriff," Shaye said. "Looks like your other one is hit but okay."

"I'll live," Winston said.

Shaye moved in among the fallen men and began checking them with Holcomb. He saw two who were alive, but blood bubbles on their lips said not for long.

"We need one man to question," he said aloud. "They're not all here. The Langers aren't here."

"There's one over here, Pa," Thomas said.

Shaye went over and stood next to his son, and was soon joined by the sheriff. They looked down at the fallen man, who was holding his hand to his side and glaring up at them. His wound seemed similar to Shaye's, except that the blood was deeper red and there was more of it. The bullet was still there.

"Pa," Matthew said, coming up next to

him, "we gotta get a doctor over here."

"Your son is right," Holcomb said.

"If you talk," Shaye said to the man, "we'll get you to a doctor."

"Fuck you."

"Where's your boss?"

"Go to hell," Red Hackett said. He'd started the whole fracas by going for his gun, and he was still alive. Shaye had no idea of the irony involved, though.

"The Langers left you here to get killed while they took off with the money."

Hackett just continued to glare.

"The money's not here, is it?"

"Get me a doctor."

"Where'd they go?"

"I don't know!" Hackett shouted. "They went upstairs a little before you hit us. Get me a doctor!"

"I'll get the doc," Holcomb said.

"Upstairs?" Shaye said, looking up. "Damn!"

He ran for the stairs, followed closely by his sons.

55

Shaye and his sons checked all the upstairs rooms. There was evidence that the Langers had been in one of them. On the floor, left behind by accident, was a twenty dollar gold piece. Shaye knew that part of the haul taken from the bank in Epitaph had included gold coins.

"The livery," he said.

He ran back downstairs, again followed by his sons. The sheriff had not returned with the doctor, and Deputy Winston was standing guard over the fallen man still holding his arm.

"Where's the closest livery?" Shaye asked.

"South end of town," Winston said, pointing. "Go outside, turn left and keep going."

"Tell the sheriff we'll be back."

They all went out the door.

When they reached the livery, the doors were wide open and some horses were wandering about. Apparently, the Langers, in a hurry to saddle their own mounts, had let some of the others loose.

"We gonna follow them, Pa?" Matthew asked.

"Not in the dark, Matthew," Shaye said. "We'll track them in the morning."

"We don't know how many there were," James said.

"Ethan and Aaron for sure," Shaye said. "If the doctor keeps that other man alive, maybe he'll tell us."

They went into the livery, rounded up some of the loose horses, and put them in stalls.

"A lot of horses," Shaye said. "Most of the gang must have boarded them here."

They left the livery and closed the doors behind them.

"We better get back," Thomas said.

"Before we do," Shaye said, "I want to tell you boys how proud I am of you. You stood up like men tonight, and none of you backed down."

Matthew and James looked embarrassed.

"Pa," Thomas said, "let's go back to the saloon. The doc's gotta take a look at you too."

"All right, Thomas," Shaye said. "Let's go."

■ ■ ■ ■

Outside of town the Langers slowed their horses, then reined them in. Morales and Branch stopped as well.

"What the hell happened back there?" Aaron demanded.

"You said there were only three lawmen," Ethan pointed out.

"Maybe they recruited some help," Branch said.

"And maybe you were trailed here from . . . what town did you hit in Texas, anyway?" Aaron asked.

"A place called Epitaph," Ethan said. "I never heard of it before, but —"

"Epitaph?" Aaron said. "You robbed the bank in Epitaph?"

"That's right," Ethan said. "It was a good haul."

"Did you bother to find out who the sheriff of Epitaph was before you hit it?"

"Well, no, but —"

"Do you remember the name Shaye Daniels, Ethan?"

"Shaye . . . yeah, from a long time ago. He was, uh . . ."

"Shaye Daniels was the best man with a gun I ever rode with," Aaron said. "I wanted him to be my partner, but he walked away."

"And he ended up sheriff of Epitaph, Texas?" Morales asked.

"That's right, as Dan Shaye."

"Madre de Dios."

"How do you know?" Ethan asked.

"Because I kept track of him, that's how," Aaron said. "I'll bet he tracked you all the way here."

"Why would he do that?" Ethan asked.

"You killed a woman," Aaron said. "Even fifteen or so years ago he had his own code. God, if that was Danny Shaye back there . . ."

They waited for Aaron to finish, but he didn't. He just gigged his horse and they moved on their way in the dark.

56

By morning people were back on the streets and things had returned to normal for the townspeople. The tension level had eased, and they were no longer worried about catching a bullet.

Sheriff Holcomb got the undertaker and some other men to clean the bodies out of the Somerset Saloon. Sam Somerset was extremely happy at having come out of the situation alive. He was offering the Shayes anything they wanted in his place for free.

All the Shayes wanted, however, was to find out how many men had fled with Ethan and Aaron Langer.

Thomas, Matthew, and James were waiting when Shaye came out of the doctor's office with Sheriff Holcomb.

"How is he?" Thomas asked.

"He died," Shaye said. "That belly wound finally got him."

"What did he say, though?" James asked.

"Nearest he can figure, the Langers got away with their *segundos,* Esteban Morales and a fella named Ben Branch."

"You know them?" Holcomb asked.

"I knew Morales a long time ago," Shaye said. "He's been riding with Aaron Langer for years. I don't know Branch."

"What are you gonna do next?" Holcomb asked.

"We'll outfit and start tracking them," Shaye said.

"Well, I can make sure you outfit for free," Holcomb said. "You may have saved this town's bank."

"I'm not sure the town owes us that," Shaye said, "but we'll take it. Thomas, you and James see to that. Okay?"

"Sure, Pa. What are you gonna do?"

"Check the horses, make sure they're sound. We've ridden them a long way."

"And me, Pa?" Matthew asked.

"Stay with me."

Shaye turned to Holcomb. "I'm real sorry about your man."

"Thanks," Holcomb said. "I guess the only silver linin' here is he had no kin."

"If there's a silver lining to having a man die," Shaye said, "I guess that's it."

"Stop into my office and say good-bye before you leave, will ya?" Holcomb asked.

"We'll do it, Sheriff," Shaye said. As the sheriff turned and walked away, Shaye said to his sons, "Okay, let's get it done, then."

Thomas and James went to the general store for some simple supplies, and talked while they shopped. Luckily, there was no pretty girl working in this store to distract them.

"How do you feel about what happened last night?" James asked.

"Relieved."

"Relieved?" James asked. "That you didn't get killed?"

"No," Thomas said, "relieved that I was so calm."

"Well, I wasn't," James said. "I was scared out of my wits. Why were you calm?"

"Because I knew this day would come, and I prepared for it," Thomas said. "And because I made every shot count. I did everything Pa ever taught us to do."

"So did I," James said. "I mean, I'm sure I missed a lot of shots, but I kept at it."

"You did good, James," Thomas said. "Pa said so."

"What did you think of how I did, Thomas?"

Thomas put his hand on his younger brother's shoulder and said, "You did great, and so did Matthew."

"I was worried about Matthew," James said.

"Yeah, I was too," Thomas admitted. "He's still not as sure about this as we are. I thought he might hesitate."

"He didn't, though," James said. "He did fine."

"Maybe this will convince him that what we're doin' is right," Thomas said. "Maybe we're all finally together on this."

Matthew was very quiet as he and Shaye checked over the horses in the livery.

"We're going to have to replace mine," Shaye said. "I think he's got some ligament damage in the left foreleg."

"Uh-huh."

"Matthew? Are you all right?"

"I'm fine, Pa."

Shaye straightened and looked at his son. "Do you have something you want to talk about? Like what happened last night?"

"Last night . . . we didn't have a choice," Matthew said. "We did our jobs, I know that."

"Then what's bothering you?"

"I killed somebody," Matthew said. "Lots of somebodies, I think. I — I just have a hard time accepting that."

Shaye regarded his son sympathetically.

Why was it that some of the biggest men —
physically speaking — were also the gentlest?

"Matthew, I never expected you to follow
in my footsteps," Shaye said. "You're not
cut out to be a lawman."

"I know that, Pa," Matthew said. He
looked down at the badge on his chest. "But
I'll wear this until we catch the men who
killed Ma, and then . . . well, and then I
don't know what I'm gonna do. Thomas
wants to be a lawman. So does James, I
think. I'll just . . . have to figure out what I
want to do."

Shaye clapped Matthew solidly on his
broad back and said, "You'll figure it out,
Matthew. We'll help you. Right now I need
you to help me pick out a horse. All we've
got to do is find the owner."

Shaye and Matthew walked the four horses
over to the sheriff's office, where they met
Thomas and James, who were carrying
burlap sacks of supplies. Shaye had chosen
a young steeldust to replace the horse with
the ligament damage. They divvied up the
supplies equally and hung bags from their
saddlehorns, then went into the office to
bid the sheriff good-bye.

"Ready to leave?" Holcomb asked.

"Moments away," Shaye said.

Holcomb came around the desk and shook hands with all four of them.

"Again, I can't thank you enough for what you did for the town . . . for me. I don't know what I would have done —"

"You would have figured something out, Sheriff," Shaye said.

"I wish you luck catching up to them," the local lawman said. "I know how important this is to you . . . to all of you."

"Thanks," Shaye said. "They won't get away from us. We'll catch them."

"If you catch up to them in this county," Holcomb said to Shaye, "in my jurisdiction, you do what you have to do. Do you understand me?"

"I understand," Shaye said. He stuck out his hand. "Thank you."

Outside, they all mounted up, and James turned to his father. "Pa, did he mean what I think he meant?"

"He did."

"What?" Matthew asked. "What did he mean?"

"He gave us permission to kill them," Thomas said.

"He did?" Matthew looked at his father.

"Yes, Matthew," Shaye said. "That's what

he was telling us."

"But . . . he's the law."

Shaye reached out and touched his son's shoulder. "He's the law, but he knows what's important, Matthew."

"We all know what's important, Pa," James said.

Shaye could tell by the look on Matthew's face that this wasn't quite true.

"Don't worry, Matthew," he said. "It'll be fine. I promise."

"Okay, Pa."

57

As they reached the outskirts of town, Shaye continued the lesson on tracking he had begun earlier.

"I'm no great tracker," he said, "but if you keep your eyes open, the terrain will tell you when someone has already passed by."

Thomas and James listened intently. Matthew, on the other hand, allowed his mind to wander. He was still thinking about the men he killed, and that he might still have to kill. His gentle spirit could not come to terms with the act of killing.

"We've also run into some luck," Shaye said.

"What kind of luck, Pa?" James asked.

"Dismount, all of you."

Thomas and James obeyed immediately. Matthew did not hear the order.

"Matthew!" James said, snapping his brother out of his reverie.

"Huh?"

"Dismount."

"Oh, yeah, sure."

When all three sons were dismounted, Shaye showed them the hoofprints on the ground. He went down to one knee, and they all joined him.

"See there?" he asked, pointing.

All three boys peered at the ground.

"What's that?" Thomas asked. "There's somethin' inside that hoofprint."

"Good eye, Thomas," Shaye said.

"What is that?" James asked.

"I'm not sure," Shaye said, "but something has either adhered to the hoof of this horse or something has caused a small amount of damage — not enough to make the horse lame, but enough to make the track unique."

"So all we need to do is keep followin' that track?" James asked.

"As long as the Langers, or whoever the horse belongs to, don't notice that they're leavin' a unique trail."

"What happens if they notice?" James asked.

"They could send the horse off on its own, leavin' us to follow a false trail."

"How can we know that?" Thomas asked.

"Well, if they send the horse off riderless, the print won't be as deep — unless they take care to weigh the animal down."

291

"There's so much involved in this," James said. "It's more . . . exact than I ever thought."

Thomas and James would pick this up quickly, Shaye knew. Matthew would have trouble with it, but it really didn't matter. If he could help it, Matthew would never again be tracking outlaws after this was over.

"The problem is," Shaye said, "it's not exact. If we follow the wrong trail, we won't even know it until we get there."

"And then what?' James asked. "What happens then?"

"Then we backtrack and start over again."

"How many men have you tracked this way, Pa?" Thomas asked.

"More than a few."

"And did you ever give up?" James asked.

"Oh yeah," Shaye said. "Sometimes it can't be helped, sometimes they get away."

"And you accept that?" Thomas asked.

"As a lawman you do," Shaye said, "because you know somewhere, sometime, another lawman will catch them . . . but this is different. As a husband — and as sons — we won't give up. I don't care how many times we have to backtrack and start again, we'll catch these men."

"But we had them," Matthew said, shaking his head. "We had them, Pa, and we let them get away."

"I know, son," Shaye said. "I know we did. And we'll have them again, and next time they won't get away."

Shaye stood up, and his sons followed, mounting their horses again.

"They're heading west," he said, "toward Hays. There's no tellin' which way they'll end up goin', though. They probably don't even know. We broke up both parts of their gangs, and they'll have to reform if they want to start again."

"What if they don't start again?" Thomas asked. "What if they have enough money now to just stop?"

"That won't happen," Shaye said.

"Why not?" James asked.

"Because there's not enough money for these men to stop," Shaye said. "Not for Aaron . . . maybe Ethan is a different story, but I know not for Aaron."

"Do you know him that well to say that, Pa?" Thomas asked.

"I knew him," Shaye said, "a long time ago. I know what kind of a man he was then."

"But you changed, Pa," James said. "You've changed since then. Why not him?"

"I've kept track of his career," Shaye said. "Maybe I wanted to see what would have happened to me if I'd stayed on that path, if I'd ridden with him. He hasn't shown any inclination to change."

"But Ethan's the one we want," Thomas said, "he's the one came to Epitaph, robbed the bank . . . killed Ma."

"They're brothers," Shaye said. "If we take one, we're going to take the other."

"Brothers," Matthew said, "like us?"

Shaye looked at his three sons and said, "Brothers, yes, but not like you. Nothing like you."

58

They rode through the night and most of the day, and then camped for the second night about ten miles outside of Hays.

"Are we goin' into Hays tomorrow?" Ethan asked.

"We can't," Aaron said. "They're bound to have sent word from Salina by now."

"Then where do we go?"

They were sitting around the fire drinking coffee. They'd finished eating, and Morales and Branch were watching the two brothers. Aaron's anger since finding out about Dan Shaye had been growing. They could all feel it.

"I don't know where you're goin', brother," Aaron said, "but I'm gonna head north, into Nebraska."

"Why north?"

"I like the North," Aaron said. "I know the country. I can get lost. I can also find some men and get started all over again."

"I like the South," Ethan said. "I could go south, through Dodge and back into Indian Territory. I could find some more men too, and start over —"

"No, Ethan," Aaron said, "when I said start over, I meant it — without you."

"Wha— What are you talkin' about?" Ethan asked. "Why? Is this about Shaye?"

"This is about stupidity," Aaron said. "You've got too much of it, brother. I can't deal with it no more. In the mornin', you go your way and I'll go mine. Morales will be comin' with me." Aaron looked at Branch. "I don't know what you want to do, Branch, but take my word for it, go off on your own."

"I can't come with you?" Branch asked.

"I don't want you."

"What about the money?" Ethan asked.

"We'll split it four ways," Aaron said. "We got four sets of saddlebags, so I'll do it tonight."

"Four equal shares?" Branch asked.

Aaron turned and looked at him coldly. "Four shares," he said.

Branch shrugged and subsided. After what happened in Salina, he knew he was lucky to be alive.

"Aaron," Ethan said, "you can't blame me —"

"I do blame you, Ethan," Aaron said. "You got Dan Shaye on our trail. Now, I don't know what kind of lawman he turned into, but he was a stubborn sonofabitch when he was riding with me, and that kind of thing don't change."

"What if I take care of him?"

"Like how?"

"What if I kill him?"

"You?" Aaron asked. "Kill Dan Shaye?"

"That's right," Ethan said. "Can we join up again if I do that?"

Aaron hesitated, then said, "I don't know, Ethan. Why don't you let me know if it happens, and then we'll see? Right now I want to turn in. You set up three watches with Branch and Morales. In the mornin' we'll split the money up and go our separate ways."

Ethan opened his mouth to protest, but Aaron wasn't listening anymore. He decided to let his older brother sleep on it. Maybe by morning he wouldn't be so pissed off and he'd change his mind.

"I'll take first, if you like," Morales said.

"Fine," Ethan said. "Wake Branch for second, and I'll take third."

"As you wish."

"What about you, Branch?" Ethan asked.

"What about me, Ethan?"

"Gonna go your separate way tomorrow, or ride with me?"

Branch thought it over only a moment. Riding alone would mean making all his own decisions — and he wasn't so sure that all that had happened was Ethan's fault . . . entirely.

"Reckon I'll stick with you, Ethan."

"Okay," Ethan said. "Okay, then. Have a pot of coffee made when you wake me for my watch."

"Sure . . . boss."

59

In the morning, Aaron Langer's anger and resolve had not waned one bit. After they'd had breakfast, broken camp, and saddled the horses, he turned and tossed a set of saddlebags to his brother, and another — somewhat less packed — to Branch.

"There's your share," he said.

"We're still splittin' up?" Ethan asked. Since his brother hadn't mentioned it, and they'd broken camp, he thought it was forgotten.

"You thought I'd sleep on it and change my mind?' Aaron asked.

"Well . . ."

"When you smarten up, Ethan," Aaron said, "maybe things will change."

"Or when I kill Dan Shaye."

Aaron smiled, but there was no humor in it. "That ain't gonna happen."

"What if it does?"

"Then I'll read about it in the newspaper,"

Aaron said, "and maybe I'll find you."

"Aaron —"

"That's it, Ethan," Aaron said. "Morales and I are heading north. I don't care what direction you head, but I'd advise you not to hit a town — Hays, Dodge, anyplace — until you get out of Kansas."

"This is crazy —"

"Maybe you should go and see Vincent again," Aaron said, mounting his horse. "Maybe he'll hide you in his church."

He wheeled his horse around and headed north with Morales right behind him. Ethan stood there a moment, stunned and puzzled.

"That might not be a bad idea, Ethan," Branch said.

"What?"

"Going back to see your other brother. Who would look for us in a church?"

Ethan looked at Branch, then said, "That might not be such a bad idea at that."

Hours later, Shaye and his sons reached the campsite, which was cold, but recently so. Thomas, James, and Matthew remained on their horses while Shaye dismounted and walked the area.

"I was afraid of this," he said.

"What?" Thomas asked.

"They split up."

300

"They're not goin' to Hays?" James asked.

"Two of them went north," Shaye said, "and two of them went south."

"Do you think Aaron and Ethan Langer stayed together?" Thomas asked.

Shaye looked up and said, "You'd think that, wouldn't you? But no, I don't think that. I think Aaron took his man and went north, and Ethan took his man and went south."

"Why?" James asked. "I mean, why do you think that?"

"Aaron's been working the North, and Ethan the South," Shaye explained.

"I mean, why do you think the brothers split up?" James asked.

Shaye, who had been down on one knee, stood up.

"Aaron is going to have to blame someone for what happened," he said, "and I think he'll blame Ethan. They probably split the money and went their separate ways."

"They're brothers and they didn't stay together?" Matthew asked, clearly puzzled.

"Maybe they get on each other's nerves a little more than you and your brothers do, Matthew," Shaye said.

He walked back to his horse and mounted up.

"So who do we follow, Pa?" Thomas asked.

301

Shaye hated to split up from his sons. Sure, they had survived their baptism of fire in Salina, but he had to decide who to send after Aaron and who to send after Ethan. He wanted Ethan because that's who had come to Epitaph, but Aaron was the more dangerous, the more ruthless, of the two. How could he send two of his sons after him just so he could have the satisfaction of killing Ethan himself?

Also, he had to split himself and Thomas up, since they were the most proficient with a gun.

"Pa?" Thomas said. "I can go north." He knew his father wanted Ethan badly. "I'll take James."

"Thomas, you take Matthew and go south," Shaye finally said. "I'll take James and go north."

"South is Ethan, Pa," Thomas said. "You said so yourself."

"I know."

Thomas looked at his father, saw a muscle pulsing in the older man's jaw.

"Aaron's more dangerous, Thomas," Shaye said. "I can't send you after him."

"Pa," Thomas said, "the three of us can go after Aaron while you go for Ethan."

That was something Shaye hadn't figured.

"Yeah, Pa," James said. "We can do it."

"Aaron and Morales are too dangerous," Shaye said after a moment. "I just can't. Thomas, take Matthew and go after Ethan. Watch for that marked hoof, it'll be easy to track."

"Yes, Pa."

"And when you catch him . . ."

"Yes, Pa," Thomas said, "I'll kill him." He looked at his brother and said, "Come on, Matthew."

"James," Shaye said, "let's go north."

60

"Thomas?"

They'd ridden in silence for a while, and Thomas knew that something was going on in his brother's head. The question would have come sooner or later.

"Yes, Matthew?"

"Are you really gonna kill Ethan Langer when we catch up to him?" Matthew asked.

"Yes, I am, Matthew."

"What if he surrenders?"

"I'll still kill him."

"Really?"

"Yes," Thomas said. "He killed Ma, Matthew."

"I know, but . . . it don't seem right."

"Don't worry," Thomas said, "you won't have to do it. I can do it myself."

They rode a few more miles in silence, but Thomas knew his brother wasn't finished.

"Thomas?"

"Yes?"

"How did you feel the other night?"

"When, Matthew?"

"When we were . . . killin' all those men."

"Matthew," Thomas said, "all those men were also tryin' to kill us, remember?"

"I know that."

"I felt good," Thomas said. "I felt relaxed, in control . . . you really want to know the truth?"

"Yeah, I do."

"For a while I felt like nothin' could hurt me that night. It was weird. And when it was all over, I felt more alive than ever."

"Really?"

"Yes."

"I just felt scared the whole time," Matthew said. "Before, during, and after. I didn't like it."

"There's nothing wrong with bein' scared, Matthew," Thomas said. "You did just fine in that saloon, just fine."

"I don't feel like I did fine," Matthew said.

"Matthew," Thomas said, "we'll be okay if you just do everythin' I tell you, understand? Just what I tell you. Can you do that?"

"Sure I can do that."

"Good," Thomas said. He reached over and slapped his brother on the back. "Good."

■ ■ ■ ■

"How's your side, Pa?" James asked.

"It's fine."

"You're bleedin'."

Shaye looked down at his injured side. He was still wearing the same bandage the doctor had patched him up with. He saw that some blood had seeped through his shirt.

"It's just leakin' a little," Shaye said. "It's nothin' to worry about."

"You ever been shot before, Pa?"

"Twice," Shaye said. "You remember that time the Jelcoe boys came to town?"

"Oh yeah," James said. "I was little, but I remember Ma patchin' you up."

"We didn't have a doctor in town back then."

"When was the other time?"

"Years ago," Shaye said, "a lot of years ago."

James decided to let it drop. He figured they'd made his pa talk about his past enough, as it was.

"How far behind are we, Pa?" he asked.

"Not far, James," Shaye said. "We'll catch up."

"Think they know we're after them?"

Shaye looked at James. "They've got to

figure someone's after them," he said. "Don't know if they know it's us."

"What would Aaron Langer think if he knew it was you?"

Shaye hesitated a moment, then said, "James, I think he'd think it was real interesting."

61

Aaron Langer stopped to take a drink from his canteen and pull out a piece of beef jerky. Morales stopped alongside him and did the same.

"I'm thinkin' there's somebody comin' behind us," Aaron said, looking off into the distance.

"Do you believe it is our old friend, Señor Shaye?" the Mexican asked.

Morales turned to look, then froze when he heard the hammer of Aaron's pistol being cocked behind him.

"Just sit still, Morales," Aaron said. He reached out and removed the man's saddlebags, containing the money.

"You are robbing me, *Jefe*?" the Mexican asked. "I have been your most loyal servant for many years."

"Yeah," Aaron said. "If you weren't makin' so much money with me, I'd like to see how loyal you would have been. Put your hands way out from your sides, Esteban."

Morales obeyed, spreading his arms like wings.

"Now turn around."

Morales swiveled back around in his saddle, stared down the black barrel of Aaron's gun.

"Are you going to kill me?"

"No," Aaron said, "you're gonna take care of whoever's followin' us. After you've done that, I'll be waitin' for you in Red Cloud, just over the border in Nebraska. There, I'll give you your money back."

"Why do you feel the need to hold my money?"

"Because if I send you off with your money, you just might keep on goin'."

"And if I say that I will not?"

Aaron touched Morales's saddlebags, which were laying across his saddle, and said, "Safer this way, Esteban. This way I know you'll do what you're told, because you want your money."

Morales stared at Aaron Langer for a few moments, then shook his head. "I thought we were *amigos*."

"When, in the past twenty years," Aaron asked, "did I ever say we was friends?"

"Never."

"Exactly. We've been a good team, Esteban, but it's only because you always did what you were told."

"*Sí, Jefe.*"

"Now, do you want your money back?"

"*Sí, Jefe.*"

"Then take care of whoever is trailing us and meet me in Red Cloud," Aaron said.

"And if no one is following us?"

"Oh," Aaron said, "somebody is, Morales. If it ain't Shaye, it's somebody. Believe me."

Keeping his gun trained on his *segundo* of many years, Aaron started his horse walking.

"I'll give you until tomorrow night, Morales," Aaron said.

"And why should I believe that you will not just keep going with my money?"

"Because then I'd have to worry about you followin' me, Esteban," Aaron said. "And you wouldn't stop until you got your money back or died tryin', right?"

"*Sí, Jefe,*" Morales said, "that is very right."

"So," Aaron said, "see you in Red Cloud."

He kicked his horse into a gallop and only then turned his gun away. Morales knew he could probably take out his rifle and pick Aaron Langer out of his saddle, but he decided not to. Why destroy a successful working relationship over one transgression?

310

Besides, if there was someone following them, it would be a good idea to deal with them now, rather than later.

Morales turned his horse south and began riding. He was reasonably sure he'd find Aaron waiting for him in Red Cloud, with his money.

62

"Pa, why would Aaron Langer go north again?" James asked. "Isn't he afraid there are posses out lookin' for him?"

"In the Dakotas, maybe," Shaye said, "not in Nebraska. But my guess is he'll head west eventually. I think he'll head for Wyoming. I don't think he's wanted there."

"Are we still trackin' him?" James asked. "Or are we just headin' north?"

"I'm trying to track him, but I told the three of you before, I'm not a great tracker. If this terrain changes, I don't know if I'll be able to see his trail. If that happens, we'll have to go back to what worked before, stopping in towns and checking to see if anyone's seen him."

"Do you think Thomas will be able to track Ethan?"

"I think so," Shaye said. "Unless Ethan changes horses, which at some point he might do."

"Then Thomas will have to go back to what worked before."

"Exactly."

Several hours later Shaye said, "I just thought of something. Damn, I wish I'd thought of it before."

"What's that?"

"Ethan," Shaye said. "He needed Aaron in order to function. If he doesn't have Aaron — I mean, if they've really split up — he's not going to be able to make his own decisions for long."

"So?"

"So if that's the case," Shaye said, "he'll head for Oklahoma City again."

"His other brother?" James asked. "The priest?"

"Yes."

"But . . . I thought he hated him."

"In the absence of Aaron, Vincent would do," Shaye said. "If Thomas and Matthew lose the trail . . ."

"Would Thomas think of that?"

"There's no reason he would," Shaye said. "It's only because I know them that I thought of it."

"Thomas won't lose him, Pa."

"I'm glad you have such faith in your brother, James." Of course, James was just telling him that to make him feel better.

There was no reason to think Thomas wouldn't lose the trail if he didn't manage to run Ethan down in a day or two — which is what Shaye was hoping to do with Aaron, simply run him to ground.

He had no idea how close they were to doing that when the first shot came.

63

James had the presence of mind to clear his saddle at the sound of the shot, but his inexperience precluded him from taking his rifle with him. Shaye, on the other hand, grabbed his Winchester before launching himself from his horse.

Both landed with bone-jarring thuds and rolled for cover behind some rocks.

"James? Are you hit?"

"No, Pa. You?"

"No."

"My horse is dead, Pa."

Shaye closed his eyes and silently thanked God for letting the bullet strike the horse and not his son. The irony of his thanking God was lost on him at that moment.

He wasn't hit, but slamming into the ground had not done anything good for his existing wound. He could feel blood beginning to soak his shirt, but he'd have to worry about that later.

"Who is it?" James called out.

"My guess is Aaron left Esteban Morales behind to ambush us," Shaye said. "It's a tactic he and Esteban have used in the past."

"Can you see him?"

"No," Shaye said. "We'll have to draw his fire again in order to pinpoint his location. That was a rifle shot, so he could be pretty far away. Do you have your rifle?"

"No," James said. "I didn't think to take it."

That was when Shaye realized that James didn't have the reflex yet to automatically grab his weapon. This also put Shaye in a quandary, once again, like in the saloon. If James were just a deputy, he'd instruct him to draw Morales's fire, since he was the one with the rifle. Even if he gave James the rifle, he wasn't a good enough shot to take Morales from where they were. Shaye didn't even know if he was going to be able to do it, or if he'd have to get closer.

There was no way around it. James was going to have to draw fire from the Mexican, who was being smart enough to conserve his ammo until he could see somebody to shoot at.

"James?"

"Yeah, Pa."

"You're going to have to draw his fire so I

316

can spot him, son."

"I figured that, Pa."

Shaye checked his rifle to make sure it hadn't been damaged in the fall from the horse.

"When, Pa?"

"I'll tell you," Shaye said. "Don't make a move until I say."

It was getting late in the day, and they were traveling north. The son was setting in the west, so it wasn't in Shaye's eyes, but it wouldn't be in Morales's eyes either.

"You're not going to be able to just pop up and down, James. You need to make him think he's got a target."

"Should I stand still," James asked, "or move?"

"You've got to move," Shaye said. "He'll hit a stationary target. When I say 'Go,' you start running to that other group of rocks over there. See them?"

"Yes," James said. He was lying on his belly where he was. "That's better cover anyway, Pa."

"Okay, then," Shaye said. "I'm not going to be able to take a shot, I'm just going to have time to spot him, and then we'll have to do it again."

"Are you gonna try to take him from here?"

"That's what I'm going to do," Shaye said. "If I can't get him, then we'll have to find a way to get closer."

"Okay, Pa," James said. Shaye detected a slight quaver in his son's voice. "I'm ready when you are."

Morales had expected to hit one of them with his first shot. He was too experienced not to know that he'd missed the men and hit one of the horses. Maybe the animal fell on the rider. That would be helpful.

He blamed his miss on the fact that he was thinking about Aaron Langer and all that money. Truth be told, he did not even know yet how much there was. They were not able to finish the tally in Salina, and when Aaron had divvied up the money into saddlebags, Morales had not had a chance to count his.

The longer he'd had to sit on his rock and wait for the riders to appear, the less sure he became that Aaron would be waiting for him in Red Cloud. After all these years of riding together, he thought that Aaron was going to try to steal his money. If that truly happened, then he was going to have to track down the man he'd ridden with for so long — given his loyal service to — and kill him. The thought did not sit well with him.

But before he could do anything about that, he had to take care of the situation. He was an excellent rifle shot. All he needed was something to shoot at. He did not know who the two men were — he was too far away to see — but they had both reacted well, quickly leaving their saddles. From his vantage point, he could not tell if they had taken their rifles or not.

He would find out soon enough, though. As he sighted along the barrel of his rifle he said softly, "Any minute now."

64

The first thing Shaye had to do was make a good guess as to where Morales was firing from. He had to pick a spot, one he probably would have chosen to use. There was a rise about a hundred yards away that would do, another beyond that about another fifty yards. He knew that a good man with a rifle could make a shot from twice that distance. Unless Morales's eyesight had gotten worse with age, he recalled him being a very good shot.

"James?"

"I'm ready, Pa."

"Okay . . . now!"

James stood up and took off running. It also made sense for him to be the target — or the rabbit — since he was younger and could run faster.

Shaye kept his eyes on the horizon and saw a man with a rifle stand up from the spot he'd chosen a hundred yards away. He couldn't tell if it was Morales, but the man moved quickly, took aim and fired, then levered a round and fired again.

Shaye, wanting to give Morales — or whoever it was — a false sense of security, fired a shot of his own that fell woefully short of its mark. Then he dropped down behind his rocks and called out, "James! You all right?"

"I'm fine, Pa." He sounded strong, though a bit farther away. "Did you spot him?"

"I did."

"I heard you take a shot."

"Just to give me an idea of range."

"Do you think you can take him?"

"I don't think I have a choice, James," Shaye said. "I've got to take a shot."

"What happens if you miss?"

"That depends on whether I miss by an inch or a mile. A mile, and he'll just stay where he is. If I miss by an inch, he'll probably hit his horse running and pick a new spot."

"If that happens you'll have to leave me behind," James said. "We'll never run him down riding double."

"Not only will I have to ride him down, I'll have to bring his horse back for you to ride. I guess I better not miss."

"Hey, Pa?"

"Yes?"

"I just thought of something."

"What?"

James hesitated, then asked, "Can he hear us?"

Shaye had to smile. "Don't worry, James. He's too far away."

"Oh, okay. Can I ask you something else?"

"Sure?"

"The longer I stay a target, the longer you'll have to get a bead on him, right?"

"That's probably right, James," Shaye said, "but don't be a hero. When I give the word, run back to where you were before, and be quick about it."

"Okay."

James would be able to do whatever he wanted, because Shaye knew there was no way he could keep an eye on his son and also take a shot at Morales.

He laid his rifle across the boulder he was using as cover, sighted along the barrel, and shouted, "James . . . now!"

James's heart had been pounding ever since the first shot was fired. When he'd made his first run, he had steeled himself for the impact of a bullet. When it didn't come, he felt great relief, but it was short-lived for he knew he would have to do it again. He was happy that his father was treating him more like a deputy in this situation and less like his son.

When his father shouted again, James sprang up and began to run back to his previous cover, but he was not moving quite as fast as he had before. He wanted to give his father time for a good shot, and maybe even a second.

He was halfway between the two areas of cover when the bullet hit him.

Morales was ready, and when the man jumped up and began running again, he took a split second more than he should have to try to lead him and make a quality shot.

As he pulled the trigger, the sound of his own shot drowned out any other sound, so when the bullet struck him in the belly, he was shocked. He staggered, dropped his rifle, and looked up in time to see the second man fire again. There was a puff of smoke from the barrel of the man's gun . . . and then Morales knew nothing. A brief moment of respect for the shooter . . .

Shaye saw Morales stagger and knew he'd hit him. In fact, the shot seemed to freeze the man where he was, so he jacked another round and fired a second, more deliberate shot.

He turned then to look for James and saw him lying on the ground halfway between the two clumps of rock he'd been running to and from.

"James!"

He dropped his rifle and ran to his son's side.

"Oh, Pa," James said, looking up at Shaye, "I think he shot me in the butt!"

65

"What's wrong, Thomas?" Matthew asked.

Thomas had dismounted and was walking around looking at the ground and then staring off into the distance. Now he walked back to where Matthew was waiting, still mounted.

"I think I lost the trail, Matthew," he said mournfully, shaking his head.

"You'll pick up the trail again, Thomas," Matthew said confidently. "I know you will. And if not, you'll figure somethin' out. You're smart, like Pa."

"Yeah, well," Thomas said, not as sure of that as his brother was, "I don't think they'll stop in any Kansas towns. Not with the word out about what happened in Salina."

"So they'll keep goin'? Back into Indian Territory?"

"Unless they head west."

"What about east?" Matthew asked.

"Too far," Thomas said, "too much of

Kansas to ride through."

"See? I told you you was smart."

Thomas took off his hat, ran his hand through his hair and looked into the distance, south.

"I'll try and pick up the trail again, but I think we should keep headin' south," he finally said. "That's where he likes to work, and that's where his other brother is."

"The priest? I thought they didn't like each other?"

"They're brothers, Matthew," Thomas said. "If Ethan decided he needed help, that's where he'd go." He put his hat on and slapped his brother's tree trunk thigh. "That's what I'd do."

"Me too."

"Okay, then." Thomas remounted. "We'll head for Oklahoma City and see if we can pick up the trail."

Thomas hoped he was making the right choice. He didn't want the killer of his mother to get away, but — and this he found odd — even more than that, he didn't want to disappoint his father, or his brothers. Matthew, he thought, was giving him much too much credit for Dan Shaye–like brains.

But Oklahoma City seemed like a good bet to him. If two brothers had split up, heading for the third brother was something a man might do. The way Thomas felt about his brothers, he couldn't imagine not going to one of them for help.

66

It had not been James's butt that caught the bullet, but the fleshy part of his hip. Shaye had packed the wound with an extra shirt from his saddlebags, and he instructed James to hold it there. Then he'd mounted and ridden out to check on Morales, to make sure the man was dead. That was something every hunt did, make sure you didn't leave a wounded animal on the loose.

When he reached Morales, the man was almost dead, but he was holding on, for some reason.

"Shay?" he said as Dan Shaye's shadow fell across him.

"Morales," Shaye said. "Where is he?"

"Red Cloud," the Mexican said. "Waitin' for me with the money."

"You think so?"

"If he's not there," Morales said, "you track him. Don't . . . let him spend my money."

"Morales . . ." Shaye said, but the man was dead.

He looked down at the body with a great degree of satisfaction, seeing that both of his shots had hit home.

He didn't bother to bury Morales. He didn't particularly care if critters made a meal of the man's corpse. He rounded up the dead man's horse, rode back to where James was, and made camp there.

The bullet in James's hip was going to have to come out.

The wound wasn't serious, but he had seen many men die from infection of a less than serious wound. A lucky break was finding a half-finished bottle of rotgut whiskey in Morales's saddlebags. Not great for drinking, but it served well in cleaning the wound out. James tried to bite his lips as Shaye poured it on his wound, but in the end he howled like a hyena and then passed out.

Now Shaye sat beside him, keeping the fire going and listening to the animals who were being drawn to Morales's corpse. He hoped none of the bigger ones would get brave and approach their fire.

While James was asleep, he used an extra shirt he'd found in Morales's saddlebags as a new bandage for his own wound, and also used the last of the whiskey to clean it out. He cinched his own bandage tight, hoping to stop the bleeding. They were alone out here, and the last thing he needed was for both of them to bleed to death.

There was no money in Morales's saddle-bags. Why had the Mexican actually allowed Aaron Langer to go on with all the money while he waited to ambush them? It made more sense to think that Aaron probably had not given his *segundo* a choice. That sounded more like the Aaron Langer Shaye remembered.

He hadn't yet told his sons that he'd once ridden with Aaron Langer, but he was pretty sure they'd figured it out by now. It had only lasted a year, and that was not a year Shaye ever thought back fondly on. He was amazed he'd been able to avoid becoming a murderer during that time. Or maybe, having watched as Aaron murdered, he was one, just by association.

He'd discussed the subject one night with Mary early in their marriage, and she had taken him into her arms and assured him that he was not a murderer, he was not responsible for what a man like Aaron Langer did.

"He would have done it whether you were there or not," she'd told him.

330

Leave it to her to always find the right thing to say.

Shaye was dozing when James suddenly came awake. Embarrassed that he had almost fallen asleep while he was supposed to be on watch, Shaye moved eagerly to his son's side. I'm *getting* old, he thought, old *and* tired.

"James? Can you hear me?"

"I hear you, Pa," James said, confused. "What happened?"

"You got shot, son."

James frowned, then said, "Oh yeah . . . in the ass."

"Not quite," Shaye said. "It's more of a hip wound."

"Oh, good," James said with relief. "Now I won't have to tell Thomas and Matthew I got shot in the ass."

"No, you won't."

James tried to move, then grimaced. "It hurts, Pa."

"I know, son," Shaye said. "It's going to hurt for a while."

"How about you, Pa?" James asked. "Are you okay?"

"I'm fine," Shaye said. "I rebandaged my wound and it's fine."

"And Morales?"

"Dead."

"You fired twice?"

Shaye nodded. "Hit him with both shots."

James's eyes went wide. "Wow!"

"I was lucky."

"Lucky with one shot, maybe," James said, "but not with two. Wait until I tell Thomas and Matthew. They'll wish they'd seen it. Heck, I wish I'd seen it."

"You did your job, son," Shaye said. "You're just as responsible for getting him as I am."

"Sure . . ." James's eyes began to flutter.

"James?"

He touched his son's face, lifted his eyelids to have a look. He'd simply fainted. Maybe he'd sleep until morning. That would be good for him.

Shaye made a decision to go to sleep himself. He wouldn't be any good the next day if he didn't. There was little chance that Aaron Langer would stumble on them, and if he built the fire up enough, it should keep the animals away.

It was a chance he knew he had to take.

67

The only thing Ethan could think to do was go and see Vincent. That meant back through Indian Territory to Oklahoma City.

"We got lucky once, Ethan," Ben Branch said. "We got through there without runnin' into any Indians. We're pressin' our luck tryin' it again, if you ask me."

"I didn't ask you, Branch," Ethan said. "You got your money, you can go your own way."

They were camped for the night about sixty miles east of Dodge City. In the morning, Ethan intended to start traveling southeast, with Oklahoma City his ultimate goal.

"Naw, I'll ride with you for a while longer, Ethan," Branch said.

"Then do it with your mouth shut."

Branch nodded, tossed some more wood on the fire.

"You take the first watch," Ethan said. "I need some sleep."

"Okay."

He rolled himself up in his bedroll, not at all sure he was going to sleep. The dead woman was in his dreams all the time now. But he knew he needed sleep or he'd be falling out of the saddle.

He thought about Aaron slapping him around in Salina. He was tired of that. Maybe it was time they split up permanently. He didn't need Aaron anyway. He'd do just fine on his own. First, though, he had to do something about these dreams. Vincent had to know something that would help, something he hadn't told him before. After all, he was a goddamn priest, wasn't he? Priests were supposed to help people. This time "Father" Vincent would help him, or he'd put a bullet in his brain.

Brother or no brother.

Branch poked at the fire, wondering why he was going with Ethan Langer. His own brother had had enough of him, maybe what he needed to do was get off on his own. Still, he'd never made the kind of money on his own that he'd made since joining up with Ethan. Maybe he wasn't the smartest of the Langer brothers, but they'd done all right. Maybe now that he didn't have to answer to Aaron, he'd get smarter.

Branch was willing to give it some time to see what happened.

But going back to see his brother the priest wasn't a good start. He hadn't been able to help him before, so what were the chances he'd be able to do it now? Actually, Branch didn't even know what kind of help Ethan thought he needed, but apparently he thought he needed it from a priest.

He looked over at the sleeping form of Ethan, who did not seem to be sleeping comfortably these days. More than once Branch had seen him snap awake and then look around him, as if to see if anyone noticed. Maybe whatever nightmare he was having was what he needed help with. A priest could help with that, couldn't he?

If they didn't get killed by Indians first.

Branch was sleepy. He was about to wake Ethan for his turn on watch when suddenly Ethan cried out and sat up. He looked around, wild-eyed, unseeing. Branch had no idea that Ethan was still deep in a dream — a dream where a dead woman was chasing him.

"Ethan —" he said, getting up and walking toward him.

Ethan continued to look around wildly, then grabbed for his gun.

"Hey, Ethan —" Branch said, alarmed. "What the hell —"

Ethan looked up and his eyes seemed to focus on Branch. Only he wasn't seeing Ben Branch. He was seeing a dead woman.

"Get away!" he shouted. "Get away from me!"

He pointed the gun at Branch, who made the mistake of freezing in his tracks. He couldn't believe that Ethan would shoot him, but before he could say a word, the gun went off. The bullet plowed into his chest, and all the strength went out of his limbs.

Jesus, he thought, as he fell to the ground, killed by a man who might not have even been awake.

The shot woke Ethan Langer up. He looked around him for the source, then realized he was holding his gun in his hand. He looked around again and saw Ben Branch lying on his back.

"Branch?"

No answer.

Ethan got to his feet, reached out toward the body, but didn't approach. "Ben?"

Still no answer.

Ethan lifted his gun and stared at it. He realized that it had been fired, but he didn't remember firing it. He holstered it, then walked over to Ben Branch. He saw that he'd been shot in the chest and was dead.

"Oh Christ," he said, not loudly. "Oh Jesus, I — I killed him in my sleep?"

He whirled around, as if someone was behind him, but there was no one there. But he thought he could hear someone laughing . . . a woman . . . a woman's laughter . . . coming from . . . where?

There it was again.

He pulled his gun and looked all around him.

"Where are you?" he called out.

This woman was going to haunt him in his waking hours now? Or taunt him?

"There's nobody there," he told himself aloud. "There's nobody there."

He holstered his gun, walked away from Branch's body, and hunkered down by the fire. There was no way he was going to go to sleep again. He poured some coffee and drank it scalding hot.

Father Vincent had to help him this time. He had to.

68

There was still enough of summer in the air that it didn't grow cold at night. This made keeping James warm easier. Shaye, although committed to sleeping, did not sleep well. He was too worried about James, and about the fire. Consequently, when James awoke that morning, Shaye had breakfast ready for him.

"Pa," James said as Shaye handed him a plate of beans and beef jerky, "this is holdin' us up. Langer is gettin' farther and farther away."

"Maybe not."

"What do you mean?"

"Morales wasn't dead when I found him," Shaye said. "He told me Aaron was waiting for him in Red Cloud, Nebraska, just across the border."

"You think he's really gonna be there? Why would Morales believe that?"

"I don't know," Shaye said. "He's dead

and we can't ask him, but it's due north of here, so that's where I'm going."

"You?" James asked. "You mean we."

"No," Shaye said, "I'll travel faster without you, James."

"You're wounded too."

"My wound won't make sitting a saddle hard," Shaye said. "Look, if Aaron is in Red Cloud, I've got to get there fast. You'll have to stay here until I come back for you."

"Pa —"

"If I don't come back," Shaye went on, "head back to the last town we passed. What was it —"

"You'll come back," James said. "I know you will."

"If I don't, just head back to that last town and see a doctor," Shaye said. "Then find your brothers. Understand?"

"I understand, Pa," James said. "But you'll be back."

"I think so too, son," Shaye said. "I think so too."

Later, Shaye saddled his horse and left all his supplies with James.

"Don't try to leave here too soon," he warned his son. "You open that wound and I'm not here to help you, you could bleed to death. I come back and find you dead, I'm going to be real angry with you."

"Don't worry, Pa," James said. "I'll be fine."

"Keep your gun close, keep the fire high at night."

"Do you really think Langer will wait for Morales?" James asked. "After all, he has both their shares of money."

"They've been riding together for a long time," Shaye said. "I just have to hope that means something to Aaron."

"Then get goin', Pa," James said. "You're wastin' valuable time."

"I'll see you in a few days, at most."

"Good luck."

"You too, son."

He hated to do it, but Shaye finally gave his horse his heels and left camp at a gallop.

Aaron Langer was sitting in a saloon in Red Cloud, a small town about twenty miles inside of Nebraska. Beneath his chair were the saddlebags filled with money. Aaron was a big enough, mean enough looking man that no one in the saloon wanted to give him a second look. He sat alone with a bottle of whiskey and a deadly glare. Some of the men in the saloon even knew who he was and didn't want any part of him.

Aaron wasn't sure why he was waiting in Red Cloud for Morales. He had all the money, didn't he? He didn't need anybody, did he? Hadn't he just cut his own brother loose?

But when it came right down to it, Morales was closer to him than Ethan ever was. And riding alone . . . well, that just wasn't something he had ever really done. There was a time in his life when he thought his partner for life might be Danny Shaye, but that didn't happen. Shaye got religion. Oh, not the way his brother Vincent had, but he got married, and sometimes that was even worse than getting religion.

So then he hooked up with Morales, and that partnership actually worked, and lasted. Not that Aaron ever told Morales he considered him his partner. They both seemed to have settled into their roles, though, and both had profited by it.

Like now, with the money that was under his chair.

Of course, if Morales never showed up, that would be okay too. The money would more than make up for it, and he could always find a new partner, couldn't he? He'd give the Mexican until tomorrow morning, and then he'd be on his way.

He looked up as a big brunette in a low-cut blue dress approached him. She had a hard-looking face but a big, soft-looking body.

"Hello, handsome," she said. "Lookin' for company?"

"Company's just what I could use, honey."

"Down here," she asked, "or upstairs?"

He grinned, forgetting Morales and Shaye. He grabbed his bottle and his saddlebags and said, "Upstairs sounds just fine."

69

Shaye rode into Red Cloud on a tired horse. He didn't even know if he'd ruined the animal, but he'd find that out later. There were other, more important things to worry about.

He encountered the livery as soon as he rode in, and decided not only to leave his horse there, but get his questions answered. The local lawman might take up too much of his time.

"Help ya?" the liveryman asked. He was long and lean, with a spring in his step. He wore sixty years on his frame real well. "Lawman, are ya?"

"That's right," Shaye said, "from Texas. Looking for a man. A man with two sets of saddlebags."

"You talkin' about Aaron Langer?"

"You know him?"

"I seen him before," the man said. "Knew somebody'd come lookin' for him when he rode in."

"What's your name?"

"Amos."

"Do you know where he is, Amos?"

"Everybody in town knows where he is," the man said. "Over to the saloon."

"Which one?"

"Ain't got but one."

"Got a lawman here?"

"Not much of one," the man replied. "He's been hidin' in his office since Langer arrived."

"Okay," Shaye said. "Thanks."

"You gonna arrest 'im?"

"That's the plan."

"He's been upstairs with Trudy all day," Amos said. "Havin' bottles of whiskey sent up, and some food. Guess mebbe they're wearin' each other out up there."

"I'm much obliged for the information, Amos."

"Just doin' my part for law and order," Amos said. "That sumbitch been ridin' roughshod over these parts for years, ain't he?"

"That he has."

"He wanted in Nebraska? I ain't heard."

"I don't know," Shaye said, "but that doesn't really matter."

Amos's eyebrows went up. "You ain't

gonna arrest him," the older man said, "yer gonna kill 'im. You got no authority here."

"Amos," Shaye said, touching his gun, "I got all the authority I need right here."

Shaye walked through town and found the only saloon with no trouble. It didn't even have a name. Folks gave him curious looks as he went, for his stride was purposeful and the look on his face said he meant business.

He entered the saloon and found it about half full. In a town that size, that was about as full as it got.

"What'll ya ha—" the bartender started to ask him, but Shaye cut him off.

"Which room are they in?"

"Who?"

"Aaron Langer and Trudy."

The man frowned. "Well, Trudy's had a fella up there with her the whole day, but I didn't know —"

"Oh, shut up, Ed," another man at the bar said. "By now everybody knows that's Langer."

"Which room?" Shaye asked again.

"Head of the stairs," the bartender said. "First room. You gonna kill 'im?"

Shaye turned and headed for the stairs without another word.

345

"If you kill him, don't make a mess!" the bartender shouted after him.

70

Upstairs, Aaron Langer was too busy continuing to satisfy a Herculean appetite for both whiskey and sex to hear anything from downstairs. The saddlebags full of money were hanging on the bedpost, along with his gun belt. Trudy was sitting on top of him, dangling her big breasts in his face and pouring whiskey from the bottle into his mouth. When the door slammed open from a vicious kick, Aaron bucked Trudy off so hard she fell from the bed. He sat up and started reaching for his gun, but stopped when he saw Shaye standing in the doorway.

"Daniels," he said. "I knew it was you."

"It's Dan," Shaye said, "Sheriff Dan Shaye, of Epitaph, Texas."

"Yeah, I know," Aaron said. He looked at the naked woman cowering on the floor. "You sort of caught me in the middle of somethin'."

"Careless of you, Aaron," Shaye said. "I

don't remember you being this careless."
He looked at the woman too. "Get your
clothes and get out."

Now that the shooting had not started
right away, Trudy got sort of brave. "He
ain't paid me!"

"You'll be paid," Shaye said. "Go downstairs and wait."

"But he —"

"Go!"

She gathered her clothes up and started
to put them on hastily as she ran out the
door.

"I didn't even know she wanted to be
paid," Aaron said. "I thought she liked me."

"Nobody's ever liked you, Aaron."

"Yeah, maybe not . . . why didn't you
come in shootin', Daniels?"

"It's Dan!"

"Okay, okay . . . Dan."

"I knew the girl was in here."

"You ain't even got your gun out," Aaron
said. "I figure I got more than an even
chance here."

"Make a move, then."

Aaron seemed to relax. "Let's talk a bit,"
he said. "Catch up on old times."

"There's no old times to catch up on
between you and me, Aaron," Shaye said.
"Your brother came to my town, robbed the

bank, and killed my wife."

"Your wife?" Aaron asked, surprised. "Jesus, he's a bigger idiot than I thought, but what's that got to do with me?"

"He learned everything he knows from you."

"You got deputies with you, Shay — Sheriff? You had some in Salina, I bet."

"My sons," Shaye said. "Three of them."

"Where are they now?"

"They're tracking Ethan."

"So you came for me alone?"

"That's right."

"I'm sorry about your wife, Sheriff," Aaron said, "but I still don't think that had nothin' to do with me. By the way, what happened to Morales? You kill him?"

"That's right."

"Too bad," Aaron said. "Me and him rode together a long time. I thought you and me were gonna ride together a long time, once."

"I got smart."

"That's what you call it," Aaron said. "Wearin' a badge for forty a month and found don't strike me as a smart move. Musta been your wife's idea."

"Don't talk about my wife."

"You ain't married no more, Dan," Aaron said, "you're a widower now. Toss the badge out the window. I got enough money in these saddlebags for two."

"No deal, Aaron."

"You takin' me in?"

"I doubt it."

"Gonna kill me for what my brother did?"

"Why not?"

"You got to be a hard man, didn't you?"

"Not so hard," Shaye said, "until lately."

"Yeah," Aaron said, scratching his hairy chest, "losin' a wife'll do that to ya, I guess."

"Enough talk, Aaron."

"Whataya want me to do? Go for my gun while my gun belt is on the bedpost?"

"That's better than the alternative."

"Which is what?"

"I shoot you right where you are."

"How would that look? An officer of the law shootin' a man while he's naked in bed?"

"I'll put your gun in your dead hand," Shaye said. "It won't make a difference, though. You'll still be dead."

Aaron's face went dead as he realized Shaye meant it.

"You're the one who said you had a better than even chance," Shaye reminded him.

"I hope my brother kills your sons," Aaron said cruelly, "and I hope his horse caved in your wife's —"

Shaye drew, surprising Aaron, who

thought he'd be able to throw the man off so he could beat him to the draw. Suddenly panicked, Aaron grabbed for his gun. He didn't know that Shaye let him get to it, allowed him to draw it before he fired his first shot. The bullet hit Aaron in the side as he was still twisted around from reaching for the gun. He grunted, but he was a bull of a man and it would take more than one shot to put him down. He kept coming around, gun in hand, and Shaye fired again. This time the bullet took him under the chin, and there was no need for a third shot.

Shaye came downstairs with both sets of saddlebags on his shoulders.

"He dead?" Ed asked.

Shaye walked to Trudy, who was dressed but disheveled. He'd already taken some money from the saddlebags upstairs, and now he shoved it into her hands. It was two handfuls and he didn't even know how much he was giving her.

"That cover the day?" he asked.

"Thanks, mister."

He headed for the door.

"Hey," Ed shouted, "is he dead?"

Shaye kept going. He figured if he got a fresh horse from the livery and rode all night, he could get back to James by tomorrow afternoon. If he didn't kill the horse, maybe late afternoon. As long as James didn't try to move, he was probably fine.

But there was still Thomas and Matthew to worry about.

"Hey," the bartender shouted, "if he's dead, you can't just leave 'im there."

Shaye was already outside so nobody in the saloon heard him say, "Just watch me."

71

Thomas and Matthew rode into Oklahoma City one week later. Thomas had been able to find enough of the distinct hoofprints to keep them on track. They had also come across one campsite in Indian Territory that showed the hoofprint, and Thomas realized that the rider was now alone.

"What does that mean, Thomas?" Matthew had asked. "Is it Ethan Langer, or the man who was ridin' with him?"

Of course, there was nothing in the cold camp that could tell them that. Thomas mounted up after inspecting the ground around the dead campfire.

"We're gonna have to assume it's Ethan, Matthew," he said. "After all, he's headed in the direction of Oklahoma City."

"If it's the wrong man, Pa's gonna be real mad."

"I think, when we explain the situation to Pa," Thomas said, "he'll understand."

"I wonder how him and James are doin'?"

"Better than we are, I hope."

"Hey, I just thought of somethin'."

"What?"

"Where are we supposed to meet up with them when we're all done?"

"Don't worry, Matthew," Thomas said. "Pa pulled me aside before we left and said that we could all find each other in Epitaph."

The thought of seeing his father and brother again, and in Epitaph, made Matthew doubly happy.

"That's good," he said, "that's real good."

Along the way they'd had one encounter with a Cherokee hunting party — five braves — just as they had their last time through the territory.

"Are these the same ones, Thomas?" Matthew asked nervously.

"I don't know, Matthew," Thomas said, "but we'll treat them the same way Pa treated the others."

Through sign language, the Cherokee indicated they were hungry. Thomas offered them some beef jerky, as he had seen his father do, but they wanted more. He ended up offering them everything else they had, but kept the beef jerky for themselves. The

Cherokee seemed to like this idea and made the bargain. They left the brothers in peace.

"Indians don't seem so bad," Matthew said, and they rode their separate ways.

"I guess nobody is, if you treat them fairly."

As they rode into Oklahoma City, Matthew said, "What do we do now, Thomas? We still don't know whose trail we followed."

"If it's Ethan's trail," Thomas replied, "he'll go to his brother's church."

"So we have to go there?"

"Not yet," Thomas said. "Let's see if we can find a place to stay near there, and a place to board the horses."

"Why don't we just go in?"

"Because Ethan is dangerous," Thomas said. "Because we don't have Pa with us and we have to do this right. If we just go walkin' in there, he might start shootin'. What if there's other people in the church? What if his brother, the priest, gets shot?"

"Okay, Thomas," Matthew said, "you're the boss. I just got one other question."

"What's that?"

"Do you remember where the church is?"

Thomas frowned, thought a moment, and said, "We'll ask somebody."

■ ■ ■ ■

Ethan Langer awoke with a start and went for his gun. He sat straight up when he realized it wasn't there. He looked around and saw he was in a room that was bare except for the bed he was on and a chest of drawers. The walls were stone, and the window a square cut out in the wall.

Was he in jail?

"What the —" he said, sitting up.

At that moment the thick wooden door opened and Father Vincent came in. "I heard you yell," he said.

"Where the hell am I?" Ethan demanded.

"You're in the church, Ethan," Vincent said. "Don't you remember? You got here yesterday."

Ethan didn't remember, and that bothered him. "Where the hell is my gun?"

Father Vincent winced at his brother's language, but said, "In the top drawer."

Ethan stood up, pulled the top drawer open, and removed his gun belt. He strapped it on and immediately felt better.

"And where are my saddlebags?"

"Bottom drawer."

Ethan opened the drawer and found the saddlebags. He opened one, saw the cash, then closed it and the drawer.

"How long have I been here?"

"As I said," Vincent responded, "you arrived yesterday. It's only been one day."

"Did I . . . say anything when I got here?"

"Only that you and Aaron had quarreled, and had gone your separate ways," Vincent answered. "I'm sorry."

"Never mind that," Ethan said. "I don't need him. What else did I say?"

"That you were still having those dreams, about the woman."

Ethan rubbed his face vigorously with his hands. "Yeah, yeah," he said, "that's why I came here. You gotta help me get rid of her, Vincent. I ‒‒ I'm startin' to hear her when I'm awake."

"She — She talks to you, Ethan?"

"She laughs at me!"

"I told you last time you were here how I thought you ought to proceed —"

"Never mind that," Ethan said. "Tell me how to get rid of her." He drew his gun and pointed it at his brother. "If you don't help me, Vincent, so help me I'll kill you."

Father Vincent stared at his brother for a few moments, then said, "I believe you, Ethan. Put the gun away and I'll try to think of a way to help you."

"You better," Ethan said. He holstered his

gun, then looked at his brother and added, "You just better."

72

Once they had their horses placed in a stable and had registered at a hotel near the church, Thomas and Matthew set off on foot. When they came within sight of the church, they stopped and discussed the best way to proceed.

"We can wait out here and see if we spot him going in or coming out," Thomas said, "but I'm sure there are other ways in and out."

"And we still don't know for sure that it's him," Matthew pointed out. "If we followed the wrong man, he has no reason to come here."

"That's right," Thomas said. "Matthew, we've got to find out if Ethan is in there, or we're wasting our time. If we both go in there, Father Vincent might warn Ethan — if Ethan's inside."

"Then how do we find out?"

"We'll ask around. Maybe somebody saw

something."

"That could take forever."

"Then we better get started."

They started to walk away, but Thomas abruptly put his hand on his brother's chest to stop him.

"What's wrong?"

"If we both leave and he's in there, we might miss him," Thomas said. "One of us has to stay here."

"Which one?" Matthew asked.

"You," Thomas said. "I'll go and check the area."

"Okay," Matthew said.

"Pick a doorway and stay hidden," Thomas said. "You're so big, you'll be noticed, but you'd be noticed going from stable to stable too."

"Okay, I'll stay," Matthew said, "but tell me one thing."

"What?"

"How do I recognize him? None of us has ever seen him, except for Pa."

That stopped Thomas cold. He'd forgotten that he and Matthew had never even seen Ethan Langer.

"Okay," he said, "we have his description from Pa, and we've seen the priest, his brother. He must look somethin' like him."

"Have you taken a good look at you, me,

and James lately? Do we look like brothers?"

"Well, James and I do bear a certain
resemblance — but that's not important.
Just keep an eye on the church. It's pretty
big, but so far we haven't seen a lot of
people around it. Maybe they only come on
Sunday. Just keep an eye for anybody goin'
in and out and I'll be back as soon as I can."

"Okay," Matthew said, "but hurry."

Thomas started away, then stopped.

"Matthew, if you think you see him, don't
approach him. Understand? Wait for me."

"I understand."

Thomas put his hand on his brother's
arm. "Don't go near him without me."

"I understand, Thomas."

"All right." Thomas took his hand back.
"I'll be right back."

"Just find that horse so we know we're in
the right place."

"If it's here," Thomas said, "I'll find it."

Inside the church, Ethan had left the back
room and walked into the church with his
brother.

"Nobody's ever here," Ethan said, looking
around the cavernous interior of the church.

"This is a very large church," Father
Vincent said, "and a very poor parish."

"Must not pay you very much."

"I am not paid anything at all."

Ethan turned and looked at his brother. "Did you see my saddlebags?"

"I told you they were in the bottom drawer."

"I know that," Ethan said. "Did you see what's inside?"

"No."

"You didn't even take a peek?"

"Not even a peek."

"There's cash in there, Vincent," Ethan said, "a lot of cash."

"Stolen money."

"Of course, but at least I have money. What do you have?"

"I have my faith," Vincent said, "and I live in the service of God."

"And you don't need money?"

"I do not need money," Vincent said, "but the church does."

"Well, don't expect to get any from me."

"I don't."

"That's good, because I don't believe in charity."

"Charity begins at home."

"Well, you finally said something I agree with."

Vincent fell silent for a moment, then said, "I have some things to do, Ethan."

"Like what?"

"I have some visits to make with the sick," the priest said. "I will be back later today."

"What about me?" Ethan asked. "What about my — my problem?"

"We will take care of it when I return," Vincent said.

Ethan grabbed Vincent's arm and held it tightly. He was surprised at how hard it was.

"Promise?"

"I promise, Ethan."

Vincent stared at his brother until Ethan removed his hand, and then the priest left the church.

Ethan sat down in the front pew and bowed his head. He wasn't praying, he was just tired.

73

Thomas decided to start asking questions
at the stable where he and Matthew had left
their own horses. First, he checked the
hooves of the other horses in the building
and found nothing. He was about to leave
when the liveryman came walking in on
him.

"Hey," he asked, "you want your horse?"

"No, thanks," Thomas said. "I've got a
question for you, though."

"What?"

"Does the priest have any horses?"

"What?"

"The church," Thomas said, "does the
church have any horses?"

"They have a buckboard and a horse, I
think."

"Do you know where they leave the
horse?"

"They got a small stable out back."

"They have their own stable?"

"Yeah," the man said.

"So if somebody was visiting the priest, they'd put his horse back there?"

The man shrugged beefy shoulders and said, "I guess so." He scratched at the sweat in his salt and pepper beard. "You visiting somebody at the church? Want to move your horse? I'll give you a discount to leave it here. Business ain't been so good."

"What can you tell me about the church?"

"Not much," he said. "It's poor, not too many people go there."

"But the place is huge."

"Yeah," the man said, "it's a big empty building."

"Except for the priest."

"Right, they got one priest."

"Okay, thanks."

"Hey, you leavin' your horse here?" the guy shouted after him.

"Yeah," Thomas said, and ran out the door.

Matthew saw the priest leave, and backed into a doorway so the man wouldn't see him. They'd only seen each other once, but Matthew knew that a man his size was hard to forget.

Once the priest was gone, Matthew thought about going inside. The church was obviously empty now, except maybe for Ethan Langer. He knew his brother Thomas was planning to do the same thing their father was planning to do — kill Ethan. But that was murder, and Matthew was still unable to accept that. If he went inside and caught Ethan Langer, maybe he could keep Thomas from becoming a murderer.

Thomas worked his way around behind the church and found the small shack they used as a stable. The buckboard was outside, and the horse was inside. In fact, two horses were inside, and when he saw that his heart began to race.

When he entered the small shack, he saw the saddle off to the side, but there were no saddlebags. He knew his father would know exactly which hoof to check, but he had to lift all four before he found the one he wanted. There was the distinct marking something had created on the horse's hoof. The odds were now distinctly in favor of Ethan Langer being inside the church.

Father Vincent didn't get very far from the church when he realized he'd forgotten his Bible, which he was going to need to offer comfort to Mrs. Anderson. He would never have forgotten it if he hadn't been so distracted by the presence of his brother. He knew the best thing he could do for Ethan would be to turn him in to the law, but he just couldn't. Somehow, he had to convince Ethan to do that himself.

He turned around and headed back. In order to get to the church, he had to pass by the small stable behind it. He thought he saw some movement inside, and went to take a look.

Matthew finally made his decision. He left the cover of the doorway and walked across the square to the church. Just outside the door, he slid his gun in and out of his holster, the way he had seen his father do a number times to be sure it wouldn't stick. Then he opened the door and stepped inside.

Thomas stood in the small stable, wondering what his next move should be. He could return to Matthew, or he could approach the church from the back and take a look inside. While he was trying to decide, Father Vincent appeared.

"What are you doing here?"

Thomas turned, and Father Vincent saw his badge and remembered who he was. The priest's heart began to beat faster.

"Hello, Father," Thomas said.

"Deputy. What can I do for you? I thought you were long gone from here."

"We were," Thomas said, "but we tracked your brother right back to here."

"My brother?"

"Ethan."

The man shrugged. "Ethan is not here."

"That's a lie, Padre," Thomas said. "I thought priests weren't supposed to lie?"

Father Vincent bit his lip.

"But brothers, they lie for each other," Thomas said. "I know, because I always used to lie for my brothers when we were kids. But we're not kids anymore, and neither are you and Ethan." He pointed. "That's his saddle and that's his horse. The horse leaves a very distinct hoofprint. See it? Almost like a star?"

Vincent did see it, and knew he couldn't lie again.

"Where is he, Father?"

74

Matthew saw the man in the first pew sitting with his head bowed. His footsteps echoed as he approached the receptacle with the holy water. Out of reflex, he was going to dip his fingers and make the sign of the cross.

At the sound of the footsteps, Ethan Langer's head jerked up. He stood and turned quickly. He saw a large man standing just inside the front doors. The sunlight coming through the stained-glass windows high above them reflected off the badge on the big man's chest.

Ethan did not hesitate. He drew and fired.

Matthew had his fingertips in the holy water when the bullet hit him in the chest, just next to the badge he wore. He grunted and took a step back. He wasn't sure what had happened. Confused, he looked down and saw the blood on his shirt. Still, it never occurred to him to reach for his gun.

He looked up and saw a man — Ethan Langer — walking up the center aisle toward him, gun in hand.

"Wait —" he said, but the man fired again. The bullet struck him in the shoulder and knocked him off balance. He staggered back, lost his footing and fell.

The man who shot him loomed over him with his gun pointed down at him.

"E-Ethan Langer?" Matthew asked, his vision dimming.

"That's right, Deputy. Why are you trailing me to hell and back over a goddamned bank in South Texas?"

"Y-You killed my mother."

"Your mother?" Ethan asked. "That stupid bitch was your mother?"

"Y-You can't call her —"

"Do me a favor, will ya?" Ethan asked. "When you see her, tell her to leave me the hell alone."

He fired one last time. . . .

At the sound of the first shot, Thomas and Father Vincent started running toward the church, each concerned for their own brother. Damn Matthew if he went inside, Thomas swore.

While they were running they heard the second shot.

"This way!" Father Vincent said to Thomas, grabbing him from behind and directing him toward a back door of the church.

As they reached that door they heard the third and final shot.

Ethan stepped over the dead lawman's body and headed for the front door. He wanted to see if there were any more outside. He opened the door and stuck his head out, but the square was empty, except for a woman and her small daughter, who were walking toward the church.

He closed the door and looked at the lawman again. At that point he heard someone rushing in from behind the altar. Quickly, he opened the door again and stepped out.

Thomas and Father Vincent ran up the center aisle toward the fallen man, each with their heart in their throat. It was Thomas, however, whose heart sank when he saw Matthew lying in a pool of blood.

"Oh, Matthew," he said, "no!"

"Oh, my God," Father Vincent said, feeling pain and relief at the same time.

Matthew had been shot twice in the chest

and once in the head. Thomas knelt next to his brother, cradled his head in his lap and began to cry.

Father Vincent knelt next to the dead man and began to administer Last Rites.

75

Father Vincent didn't get very far with the Last Rites because they heard a woman screaming and shouting from outside. Thomas didn't want to leave Matthew, but he gently laid his brother's head back down on the floor and ran to the door, followed by the priest. Outside, a woman was screaming and wringing her hands.

"Mrs. Paul," Father Vincent said, "what is it?"

"A man," she said, "a man came out of the church with a gun and took my daughter."

"Jenny? He took Jenny?"

"Yes, yes," she said, still wringing her hands, "he took her. Why did he take her?"

Vincent looked at Thomas. "She's six," he said, "six years old."

Thomas looked at the woman. She was faded, looked too old and worn-out to have a daughter that young.

"Which way did he go?" Thomas asked.

"Across the square," she said, pointing. "He ran across the square, draggin' my baby —"

"Stay with her," Thomas said to the priest, "and with my brother."

"But —"

Thomas didn't wait any longer. He drew his gun and started running. Father Vincent was caught in a quandary. There was a dead man on the floor of his church, Mrs. Paul needed comforting, and a man was chasing his brother with the goal of killing him.

Like any man with too many options, he just froze.

Ethan had his gun in his right hand and the little girl on his left. He alternately dragged her and lifted her off the ground. Either way, she kicked and screamed for help. People were getting out of his way, pointing and shouting, and he knew he was leaving an easy trail to follow. No one made a move to try and stop him, though. The people in this city were the same as the people in Epitaph had been. No one would step up and lend a hand, try to help.

He'd had no time to think about killing the lawman. Would killing the son get rid of the mother who was haunting him? He didn't know. Had Vincent, his own brother, sent the law after him, after making an excuse to leave the church? He didn't know that either. He didn't know much, and he especially didn't know where he was running to.

He wished the girl he was carrying would stop screaming.

Ethan was leaving an easy trail for Thomas to follow. In fact, people pointed the way, helping him follow in Ethan's wake. Also, as he got closer, Thomas could hear the girl screaming. He tried to put the sight of Matthew lying dead on the floor of the church out of his mind and just concentrate on catching Ethan — the man who had killed both his mother and his brother.

Ethan staggered in the middle of the street now, unsure of which way to go. He held the girl tightly, trying not to pay attention to her screaming, but it was echoing in his ears, and it seemed to be in unison with the screams that were already there.

"Stop screaming!" he shouted, turning in circles. "Stop screaming, damn it!"

He wasn't only shouting at the little girl.

Thomas turned a corner and came to an

375

abrupt stop. Ethan was standing in the middle of the street, waving his gun, holding the squirming little girl in his hand like a rag doll, shouting, "Stop screaming! Stop screaming!"

The poor girl's head bounced around as he shook her. Her arms and legs were flapping about.

Thomas stopped, also in the middle of the street, and pointed his gun. All the riding, all the searching, all the death had led up to this moment.

"Ethan Langer!"

Ethan didn't hear Thomas shout at first, because the girl was still screaming, and there was screaming going on in his head. It was as if the dead woman was right in his ear, screaming along with the little girl. The two of them were making his head feel as if it was going to explode.

Then, abruptly, he heard his name, and there was silence.

For some reason, the little girl fell silent, and the entire street was quiet. People had fled to the sidewalks or ducked into buildings to watch from windows. There were only three people on the street now — Ethan Langer, Thomas Shaye, and Jenny, the little girl.

Ethan turned at the sound of his name, holding the girl in front of him, her feet dangling in the air. "Who are you?" he shouted. "Another deputy?"

"That's right," Thomas said. "I'm a deputy, and you killed my mother, and my brother."

"Another brother?" Ethan asked. "Jesus, am I gonna get to kill your whole family?"

"I don't think so, Ethan," Thomas said, "because it all ends here. This is the deputy who gets to kill you. Let the girl go."

"Wait," Ethan said, cocking his head. "Do you hear that?"

"Hear what?" Thomas asked.

"That . . . that laughter," Ethan said, looking around. "First she screams, and then she laughs. Your goddamn mother was haunting my dreams, but now I hear her when I'm awake."

"That's because that's what you deserve," Thomas said. The man must have been going mad, but that was no excuse for the things he'd done or for what he was doing now. "To be haunted the rest of your life — which isn't going to go on much longer."

Ethan brought his gun hand up to the side of his head and pounded on his ear.

"Get out of my head!" he shouted. "Get

out, get out, get . . . out!"

For a moment Thomas thought the man was going to shoot himself in the head, but it didn't happen.

"Ethan!" Thomas shouted. He wanted to be heard over his mother's voice, which Ethan was obviously still hearing. "Let the girl go." Thomas pointed his gun, but Ethan was holding the girl high, and she was blocking his torso. Thomas had two targets — Ethan's legs. He could have tried for a head shot, but the girl's head was partially blocking that as well. If he tried, he might end up killing the little girl.

"Ethan! Put her down!"

There was no doubt in Thomas's mind that he was going to take a shot. He kept trying to get Ethan to let the girl go, but either way it was going to end here. Ethan Langer was not going to get off this street alive. If he didn't kill him, how would he ever explain that to his pa?

"Goddamn it!" Ethan shouted. He pointed his gun at Thomas. "You wanna kill this little girl? You go ahead and take the shot. What're ya, afraid?"

In the end, Thomas took the shot not to save the little girl's life, but to save his own. Ethan had his gun pointed at Thomas and was obviously ready to pull the trigger.

Thomas had no intention of just standing there and letting the man kill him. He'd already killed too many members of the Shaye family.

Thomas lowered the barrel of his gun and fired. His bullet hit Ethan in the right shin, completely shattering the bone. There was an explosion of blood, soaking the dirt beneath Ethan's feet. The outlaw howled in pain and released the little girl. He fell to the ground, grabbing for his shin, dropping his gun. The girl ran toward Thomas, her arms outstretched.

Thomas dropped to one knee and caught her in his arms.

"Are you all right, sweetheart?" he asked. He held her at arm's length and looked her over. She seemed unharmed.

She nodded. He thought she must be a brave little girl, because she wasn't crying. She grabbed him, though, and hugged him tightly, and he hugged her back for a few moments before holding her at arm's length once again.

"You go and wait for me over there by that building," he told her, "and then I'll take you to your mother. Okay? I promise. Just stay there and wait."

Reluctantly, the girl left the safe haven of Thomas's arms and went to wait for him.

Thomas got to his feet and walked to where Ethan was rolling around on the ground, both hands bloody from his leg.

"You crippled me, damn it!" the outlaw shouted. "You sonofabitch, you crippled me."

His gun was lying in the street, so Thomas gave it a good kick and sent it skittering away. Then he pointed his gun at Ethan's head.

Ethan glared up at him, both hands wrapped around his shattered leg, and said, "Do it! Do it, goddamn it!"

Thomas's finger tightened on the trigger. This was what it all came down to.

"Go head, put me out of my misery," Ethan said. "She's never gonna stop, she'll never leave me alone, will she?"

"No," Thomas said, "she won't."

"Then kill me, damn it."

Thomas was a hair from pulling the trigger when he suddenly lowered the gun. He fired once more, shattering the other leg. Ethan screamed.

"What are you doin'?" Ethan cried out.

"You're goin' to jail, Ethan," Thomas said. "You're goin' to Huntsville. There, as a cripple, you'll be fair game for anyone who wants to have at you, and my mother will be in your head all your waking and sleeping hours." Thomas holstered his weapon. "Why would I want to save you from that?"

Beyond Ethan, Thomas could see policemen rushing toward them. He turned and walked back to the little girl, leaving Ethan for them to handle. He was going to take the little girl back to her mother, and care for his brother.

"Ya can't kill me because you're yella!" Ethan was shouting at Thomas. "Yer yella, like your brother! Come back here and kill me! Come back here. . . ."

76

Dan Shaye, Thomas Shaye, and James Shaye stood at Matthew's gravesite. Matthew was being buried right next to his mother. Townsfolk were once again gathered around the men.

It was a week later and Ethan Langer was in custody. He had not yet been sentenced, but he would be, and he'd spend a lot of time — the rest of his life, probably — in Huntsville Prison. Before he died, the voice in his head would probably drive him crazy. This was a concept Thomas had been able to embrace, but he had not yet been able to convince his father. The older Shaye was still upset that Ethan Langer remained alive.

Thomas had not had time to leave Oklahoma City with his brother's body before Shaye and James met him there. Shaye had decided, after killing Aaron Langer, the same thing Thomas had decided — that Ethan would go to his other brother, Father

Vincent. He had retrieved James from the campsite he'd left him at and taken him to the nearest town, where a doctor treated him. He then put him in a buckboard to transport him to Oklahoma City.

When they arrived, they went directly to the church, where they found Father Vincent. He told them what had happened and that they could find Thomas in a nearby hotel. Stunned into silence, Shaye drove the buckboard to the hotel and helped James down from the back of it. They went inside and asked for Thomas's room number.

Shaye left James in the lobby, visibly shaken, seated on a sofa, while he went up to Thomas's room. His oldest son opened the door to his knock and fell into his arms, sobbing.

"I'm sorry, Pa," he said, "I'm s-so sorry. . . ."

Shaye hugged his son tightly and said, "It's not your fault, Thomas. If it's anybody's fault, it's mine. I should never have brought you boys along."

Thomas cried himself out, since he had not been able to do so until then. Shaye held his son with unrestrained relief that he, at least, was alive and unhurt.

"Come on," Shaye said, patting Thomas

on the back consolingly, "James is down-stairs. He couldn't come up because he got shot in the hip. You see? His getting shot was my fault too."

"No, Pa," Thomas said. "We all wanted to come with you. Ma's dead, and Matthew's dead, and the only one to blame is Ethan Langer."

"Well . . . and he's dead, right?" Shaye asked. "You killed him?" Father Vincent had not told Shaye the entire story.

"No, Pa." Thomas drew away from his father's embrace and set himself for Shaye's anger. He hung his head and waited for it.

"What?"

"I-I didn't kill him."

"Why not?"

"I shot him in the legs. . . ." He explained how Ethan Langer was hiding behind a little girl, and how he had taken the only shot he had. How he'd shot Ethan in both legs in order to leave him a cripple, and he explained about the voices in the man's head.

"But after you shot him, and he let the little girl go, why didn't you kill him?" Shaye asked, confused. "You know that was the whole point — to kill him. If you didn't kill him, your brother died for nothing. Your mother's death goes unavenged."

"Pa, let me explain —" Thomas begged.

"Come downstairs," Shaye said. "You can explain it to your brother at the same time. I'm sure he'll want to hear it too."

Shaye turned and walked stiffly away from Thomas. He was feeling many things — shock, dismay, anger, and confusion. Thomas closed the door of his room and followed his father to the lobby.

After he explained his decision to his brother and his father, Thomas took them to the undertaker's, where Matthew was waiting. They went in to see him together, but after a few moments Shaye said, "Would you boys leave me alone with your brother, please?"

"Sure, Pa," Thomas said.

He took James outside and allowed his younger brother to cry on his shoulder.

Inside the undertaker's parlor, Shaye looked down at his middle son. The bullet holes were bloodless now, and that seemed to make them look more invasive. Matthew, the gentlest, kindest of men . . . even the way he died indicated that. Thomas told Shaye that Matthew's hand was still wet from the holy water. Ethan had to have shot him while he was dipping his fingertips. Matthew never had a chance.

Shaye took his son's cold hand in his and

said, "I'm sorry, Matthew. I'm so sorry, boy. Go to your mother, now. She'll take care of you better than I did."

They brought Matthew's body back to Epitaph in the buckboard, to be buried next to his mother. James was recovering well from his wound, walking with a cane, which he leaned on now by the gravesite.

There were no badges on the chests of any of them now. Dan Shaye had gone to Mayor Garnett's office upon their arrival and turned in all four badges.

"You don't want to do this, Dan," the mayor had said.

"Yeah, I do," Shaye said, and that was all. He walked out of the office, no longer a lawman. He also sold the house, so they'd have some traveling money and might be able to settle somewhere else. He just didn't want to stay in Epitaph any longer. The memories were too painful. He couldn't spend his days protecting these people when they had done nothing to protect themselves, nothing to protect his wife. He gave them back the money for their bank and made the bank manager promise to send the rest of the money back to the bank in South Dakota that Aaron had robbed. He wanted nothing more to do with Epitaph.

386

"But, Pa," James had complained, "this is where Ma and Matthew are."

"Son, they're buried here," Shaye said, "but they're in our hearts, and they'll go wherever we go."

"But, Pa —"

"James, you're a grown man, and so is Thomas. Either of you can go or stay as you please. I'm leaving, and that's all there is to it. The rest is up to you."

James wanted Thomas's support, but his older brother had not recovered from the responsibility he felt for Matthew's death. He had no opinion. He was willing to stay or go, whatever their father decided, so James figured to do the same thing.

This time, when Dan Shaye dropped a handful of dirt into the grave, he contrived to miss the coffin. He did not want to hear the sound of the dirt hitting it. It was still too loud from the last time.

Folks came to the funeral and the burial, but as they filed past Shaye and his two remaining sons, they received the same acknowledgment they'd received the first time — none. These people, once his neighbors, were nothing to Dan Shaye now. Looking at them only reminded him of how gutless and ungrateful they were.

They waited until everyone had left and the grave digger started shoveling dirt into the grave. The three of them had their horses waiting at the base of the hill, and two packhorses with supplies. Wherever they were going, they were not in a hurry to get there.

As they walked down the hill with their father leading the way, Thomas and James walked alongside each other right behind him.

"He hasn't spoken to me since we got back," Thomas said. "No more than three words, anyway."

"You did the right thing, Thomas," James said.

"Do you think so?"

"Yes," James said. "The way you explain it, I would have done the same thing. That man will suffer the rest of his life now, and then he'll burn in Hell afterward. It's what he deserves."

"Pa don't see it that way," Thomas said. "He still wants him dead."

"Pa can't get to him while he's in prison," James said. "Don't worry, he'll come around. Pa will forgive you, Thomas. You'll see."

"I don't know, James," Thomas said. "I don't know if he ever will."

■ ■ ■ ■

They left Epitaph right after the burial, straight from the cemetery. None of them knew where they were going, all they knew was that they were leaving Epitaph.

The employees of Thorndike Press hope you have enjoyed this Large Print book. All our Thorndike, Wheeler, and Kennebec Large Print titles are designed for easy reading, and all our books are made to last. Other Thorndike Press Large Print books are available at your library, through selected bookstores, or directly from us.

For information about titles, please call:
   (800) 223-1244

or visit our Web site at:
   http://gale.cengage.com/thorndike

To share your comments, please write:
   Publisher
   Thorndike Press
   10 Water St., Suite 310
   Waterville, ME 04901